To Dad,
who put success within the reach of two indigent brothers,
with apologies for making you such a mean SOB.

PROLOGUE

On the edge of twilight, the island of Kauai juts up like a green and gold beacon. At the tip of one of the greenest knolls stands a grand estate. The late rays of the sun reflect from it like alabaster.

The sun is settling in the mountains behind Kalihiwai Ridge, giving the sky a brilliant orange cast. As the two men watch, the ocean below is slowly changing from its daytime blue to striking shades of purple. They can hear the surf breaking at the foot of the cliffs. Across the wide lawn comes the evening chatter of tropic birds. A lone hang-glider silently drifts overhead, lazily riding the air currents from the distant peaks to the shore below. The trade winds rustle in the palms near them and cool the brothers as they sip their traditional early evening brandy.

Out beyond sight of land, the Pacific churns in eddies and currents, dispersing the last remains of Raymond Mosier. Mark and Craig Mosier had just returned from spreading their father's ashes at sea off the Na Pali Coast. Ray Mosier had turned 88 last month and had lived to see the new millennium—the year 2000. His sons had seen each year pass with increasing wonder. The old man's heart had only seemed to get stronger, but in the end it could not save him from his massive cerebral hemorrhage.

At the men's feet were several cardboard boxes Ray had squirreled away in his attic, probably more than thirty years ago when he moved to the island. The brothers had not known of their existence and had no idea what they might contain. They had just begun to sort through the material and were leisurely reliving the past, filling in gaps bit by bit and making new discoveries about their father—and themselves.

Craig had just opened a small box of loose photographs, all black and white, many faded, obviously dating back many years. The one he held had a wide white border with an ornately scalloped edge.

"Why do you suppose Dad put these away?" he asked, stroking his well-trimmed, white beard. "Look at this—it's a great shot of the old Water Street house I've never seen!" He stretched his arm sideways and handed the

5

memento to his brother.

Mark studied it in awe. Finally he said, "He never was into photo albums, I guess. This is a beauty—see what else he's been hiding from us all these years!"

Craig reached in and withdrew a yellowed snapshot, lifting his glasses to inspect it more closely. "Looks like our yard, and we're playing a game— *croquet!* And there's Tito going after the ball." Tito had been the family dog, beloved by Mark and Craig.

"Remember how that used to infuriate Dad?" Mark recalled.

"Do I! In fact, once he kicked him so hard he broke his ribs, and we had to leave him at the vet's—"

"My God, Craig!" Mark cut in. "Let me see that photo!" He tore the picture from Craig's fingers. Then, "See if you can find any more of the croquet game!"

Craig rifled through the loose prints and handed Mark two more shots of the family engaged in the venerable lawn sport.

Mark counted: "Four, five, six—*yes!* We were all playing, see?" For Craig's benefit, he pointed out the six family members. Each held a croquet mallet.

"Jesus!" Craig whispered hoarsely. "You mean—it's the day Dad kicked Tito?"

"The day Dad kicked Tito," Mark echoed. "Our last croquet game."

"But how do you know?"

"Don't you remember? Tito wasn't there when…." Mark trailed off, but Craig knew.

Both men were boys again, as shared memories made them captives once more of their youth. There was no choice; they simply had to let the events replay themselves.

PART I

1

The metallic clang of the noon school bell burst upon the empty silence of the playground in sudden urgency, as if it were intended to awaken the dead. It echoed across Steven's Field and, in only slightly diminished decibels, reverberated through the length of Lincoln Grade School. The intensity of the jangle was hardly necessary, anticipated as it was by the youngsters.

It was 1952. Teachers at that time still commanded enough authority to hold their charges in their seats until dismissed. Once given their leave, of course, it was generally pandemonium; the rule prohibiting running in the hallways, while having been the subject of more than one "general assembly," proved utterly impossible to enforce. Freedom once given could not be confined.

Mark Raymond Mosier crouched in his escape position, books already gripped securely under his left arm, right arm on his desk ready to catapult him toward the door. He would have to hurry if he wanted to beat his little brother to the bike rack. Why was it that his class was always the last to be excused?

Mrs. Ralston was pointing a raised eyebrow in Mark's direction, and he relaxed. *Dadgummit!* he thought.

In the sixth grade, Mark was already bigger than some grown men, not only tall and broad-shouldered, but with an unusually heavy physique for his twelve years. He had inherited the strong, square jaw of the Mosier men, and it was now firmly set, teeth clenched. Below his well-combed shock of charcoal hair, a pair of deep-set hazel eyes winked in alert expectation. He was normally friendly, but his mood could change quickly. His smaller classmates all knew what to look for: when angered, Mark's eyes flashed green, and it was time to get out of his way.

The story went that once Mark had been goaded about his size, ganged up on by a group of smart alecks—some said six, some more—but he had not wanted to fight. When they had persisted and begun calling him a coward and a big sissy and crowding around him, several of the boys saw the unmistakable flash of green in Mark's eyes. In the next furious instant Mark had raged among them and crumpled them like September cornstalks. One boy, apparently of the mind that there was an inverse relation in size to fleetness of foot, threw one last taunt at Mark as he took off at a trot. The other boys sat on the ground and watched as Mark stretched his powerful legs and outdistanced his prey, bringing him to justice. And most of the time, Mark was fair and just and did not abuse his power. Thenceforth he had been treated with a healthy respect.

Mark saw the moment approaching and stopped blinking, eyes intent on Mrs. Ralston. The nod came.

Many in the class had missed it, or just didn't care. Mark reached the door before most were on their feet, prompting the teacher to call his name. She might have saved her breath.

"See you after lunch, Mrs. Ralston!" Mark was out the door and into the already crowded hallway, and nothing more could be heard above the clamoring, hungry throng.

Mark had to fight his way into the onslaught of kids heading in the opposite direction, toward the cafeteria. He was glad that, since getting their bicycles, he and his brother no longer had to wait in that blasted line for cardboardy meatloaf and pasty mashed potatoes, or try to eat while surrounded by the mindless din of uncompromising youth. Instead, they were heading home for the likes of Campbell's tomato soup—with Ritz crackers, of course—and Velveeta cheese sandwiches. It was a feast for their simple tastes, but most important of all was the fact that it was served with the most extraordinary loving care by their mother.

Mark was quite pleased with his progress and thought he just might win this time. But as he reached the stairs leading from the east exit to the bike rack, there was Craig, sporting a look of disdain. How did the little twerp do it?

Craig Stanfield Mosier was so small that his brother could walk up behind him and, stooping slightly, place his chin atop Craig's head. He had finely chiseled features: a small, straight, perfectly formed nose, cheeks as smooth as freshly sculpted clay, and exquisitely proportioned forehead and eyebrows, below which grew inordinately long eyelashes. His tousled, curly brown hair grew well down the front of his scalp and out on his temples, where it nearly joined the edges of his eyebrows.

Craig's wonderful nose was now all but hidden behind the new eyeglasses he had to wear as the result of a fifth-grade eye test—his first ever. The classroom itself had been used for the examination, set up in such a way that the student sat at the front of the class, facing the back where the examiner stood by an easel. On the easel were placed white placards with rows of black letters for identification. No one seemed to be having any trouble, but when it was Craig's turn, he could not read them.

The eyes of his classmates were all on him as he squinted down the aisle in the middle of the room. Heart pounding, he guessed, pulling letters out of the air. Snickering came from several familiar sources and Craig felt his cheeks and ears flush with heat. Other placards with increasingly large letters were substituted. Guessing wrong again and again, he finally heard the examiner exclaim, "Well, maybe you can see *this!*" She rummaged at the back of the box of placards and put up the giant "E." At this a murmur of laughter coursed through the class, adding to Craig's misery momentarily, for soon the laughter turned to gasps of incredulity. For not even the largest letter in the examiner's arsenal could he correctly identify, nor when it was reversed, could he say with certainty which way it pointed. The examiner had looked at Mrs. Johnson; Mrs. Johnson had shaken her head and looked sadly at Craig.

Craig knew what it meant: his hopes for being a jet pilot were dashed; he could probably forget about the lumberjack idea; glasses would force him to be someone other than himself, less adventuresome, more vulnerable.

But it wasn't all bad. He could see the leaves on trees—from even far away—and read the blackboard from anywhere in class, not just the front seats. And, most notably, on the day he had first returned to class wearing his glasses—expecting to be greeted by ridicule (only one other classmate wore glasses, and he was blind in one eye)—Nancy Puddles had smiled sweetly at him and said: "Oh, Craig—you look sooo *cute* with glasses!"

So it was that Craig thought he might adjust to the idea—the necessity— of wearing glasses every moment of his waking life. Still, it would be some time before he grew enough so that the bridge of his nose could support the weighty glass lenses of the day. Whenever Craig would register surprise of any sort, the confounded things would suddenly slide down his nose in the most obvious and haughty manner, as if he were some ancient sage passing judgment on events.

"Hurry up, Mark! It's about time—we only have an hour!" Craig said impatiently.

"Shut up, stupid!" Mark balled his fist, walked deliberately up to little Craig, and pounded him several times on the shoulder. Craig was used to this treatment from his big brother and fancied himself tougher for it.

Having reestablished the brotherly hierarchy, they mounted their trusty steeds—Mark his big Schwinn, affectionately named "The Yacht," Craig his nondescript "Sagebrush"—and set out at full speed. They flashed by the Red & White store, the maple grove, the museum, the trail down the hill to The Point. Before them lay Water Street and the neighborhood that encompassed almost their entire world. Just three more blocks and they'd be home.

. . . . .

Victoria Ann Mosier had just turned thirty-eight yesterday, April 24th, 1952, and was one of Olympia's acknowledged beauties. She had been asked to model for local fashion shows a number of times. She was tall, with perfectly formed limbs and a tiny waist. Full round breasts accentuated the sensual swell of her hips and completed the exquisite symmetry. Her lovely face was demurely framed in dark waves of rich, black hair.

A warm, loving person, Vicky walked a dangerous line between her explosive husband Ray and the children who meant life itself to her. Before the war, he had been so gentle. She often wondered what had happened in the war to change him. Now she was forever the peacemaker, having to cajole Ray on the one hand, diverting his wild outbursts, while at the same time reassuring the children of his love for them.

Mark and Craig adored her.

Vicky had just put the soup on the stove when she heard steps on the back porch. *Another visitor,* she thought, *one of those hoboes from the tracks below the capitol buildings.* They often came by, asking for food; it had become common since the war (unknown to the family, she had taken pity on them and normally invited them in to eat). *I'll have to turn him away—the boys will be home any minute.*

. . . . .

Turning onto Water Street, Craig cut the corner on Mark and took the lead.

. . . . .

The knock came. With a sigh, Vicky opened the door. Before her stood the most pitiful character she had seen yet: sad eyes blinked at her behind dirty strands of dangling hair, white stubble of beard, clothes that were no more than rags, tattered hat gripped tentatively, hopefully, against his chest. How could she possibly turn this forlorn creature away?

"Got any jobs, missus? I could shore use some grub."

Vicky's resolve melted. "Do you like soup?" she asked.

. . . . .

"Darn you, Craig!" Mark roared, kicking at his brother's bike, almost sending him into a nearby holly tree. Craig lost momentum and Mark pulled even.

. . . . .

The hobo sat at the kitchen table rudely slurping from his bowl of tomato soup. As he finished, he kept the bowl raised, staring over the rim at his comely hostess. And what a looker she was! Her short, full skirt played about her knees. Her black-seamed stockings over her shapely legs stirred long-forgotten cravings within him. At this moment, she bent low to open the bottom drawer and rummaged through the contents for some utensil. He caught the enticing view of her exposed white thighs above her stockings, and the garters ascending to forbidden heights.

. . . . .

Now Craig was mad, and by furious effort he managed to move slightly ahead. He jockeyed for position to beat Mark into their driveway. But Mark had taken one of his famous shortcuts across the lawn, and as it happened they entered the garage in a dead heat.

. . . . .

CRASH!

The soup bowl slipped from the hobo's fingers as uncontrollable urges rose in his groin. Vicky jumped at the sound and swung around as he lunged toward her. She screamed, and he was on her, ripping her clothes off, trying to silence her with a huge hand, hurting her. His hot whiskey breath overwhelmed her.

. . . . .

They heard the soup bowl crash.

"What was that?" Mark said with alarm.

A choked scream reached their ears and the race home was forgotten.

"Hey, that's Mom!" Craig's voice broke.

"Let's go! Shhh!"

They crept silently up the stairs onto the back porch and approached the kitchen door cautiously. Mark looked through the window.

The hobo had Vicky bent back across the counter, with one forearm across her throat, choking the life out of her. His pants were down around his knees, and his free hand was fumbling around his groin.

Without thinking, Mark grabbed a croquet mallet from the old set that always sat there on the back porch when it wasn't in use, and burst in the door. Craig, who always followed his brother, grabbed another mallet and ran in behind him, his glasses slipping down his nose.

The hobo, hearing the door bang open, whirled around, releasing Vicky, who slipped senseless to the floor. There he was in full view, his hairy genitals swinging to and fro.

Both boys stopped short at the vulgar sight, and Craig—before Mark even had time to think—blindly swung his croquet mallet in a horizontal arc, clopping the swollen obscenity in front of him right across its ugly purple head.

The hobo dropped to his knees with a high, whistling shriek, cupping his hands, but not daring to touch himself. By this time, Mark—eyes flashing green—had got his wits back about him, and put his not-inconsiderable bulk into a nearly 360-degree swing that hit the hobo in the center of his forehead with a sickening crunch, splintering the mallet and sending the hobo flat on his back.

The hobo's eyes stared vacantly at the ceiling. Little red bubbles trickled from the corners of his mouth. A thick blob of dark blood oozed from his crushed skull.

The hobo was dead.

2

Craig dropped his mallet and gasped, "Mom!" He scrambled over to where she lay crumpled on the floor.

"Wait!" whispered Mark. "I think she just fainted."

"Yeah, she's breathing." Craig sighed with relief. "And I don't see any blood."

"Whew!" Mark exhaled. "We've gotta get him out of here before she comes to!"

"What for?" Craig wanted to know.

"Because Mom and Dad can't ever know about this, stupid!"

"The Playhouse!" Craig blurted out.

"That's it!" Mark agreed.

The Playhouse, sitting on the edge of the woods, was the boys' very own sanctuary. Nobody except Mark and Craig was ever allowed entry without their permission. Their dad had made this promise years ago and the brothers meant to keep it that way. It was the perfect place for hiding something.

Feverishly, they began dragging the dead hobo feet first toward the open kitchen door. "Pull, Craig!"

He was heavy, and now the boys understood the meaning of "dead weight." It took every ounce of their strength to heave the body through the door onto the back porch.

"Lookit all that blood," Craig panted.

"Hurry! We gotta get back here and clean all this up!"

Each grabbing a leg, they pulled the corpse down the rickety wooden steps. *Thump-thump-thump!* went the head as it bounced down each step.

A seemingly insurmountable distance lay between them and the outbuilding—it had never looked so far away! Dazed but determined, they wrestled with the inert man until they had him safely stowed inside The Playhouse.

They took a few seconds to gather their thoughts. "We'll have to bury him somewhere pretty soon," Mark said slowly.

"Why?" asked Craig.

"'Cuz he'll start to smell, stupid!"

Craig considered this.

Recalling their immediate crisis, they jumped up, secured The Playhouse door, and sprinted for the house.

"Oh, good, she hasn't come around yet. I'll grab some towels," said Mark.

"She'll know if we use her nice towels," suggested Craig. "Let's get the rag bag."

"Oh, yeah!"

The boys set to work mopping up the bloody kitchen.

"Make sure you get it all!" Mark ordered, scrubbing frantically.

The minutes passed. As they were finishing, there came a faint sound from their mother.

"Quick, Craig! Throw the rags in The Playhouse! She's waking up!"

"What about the mallets?" Craig reminded him.

"Put yours back in the rack. Take the broken one out with the rags."

Craig ran as fast as he could, trying not to cover himself with blood in the process. When he returned to the kitchen, Mark was placing a dripping washcloth over Vicky's brow. Embarrassed by her nakedness, he sent Craig for a blanket.

"Are you okay, Mom?"

"Wha—what happened?" she croaked faintly. Mark could barely hear her.

"The hobo. Remember?"

She made a soft cry, looking down at herself. One pink breast lay exposed and her torn skirt revealed her lovely thighs to her son, who was making every effort not to look. Just in time, Craig arrived with the blanket, ending their dilemma. *Thank goodness!* Mark thought.

"Where is he?" Fear shone in her eyes once more. "Are you boys all right? What happened?"

"We took care of that guy. He won't be bothering you again, Mom!" Craig said proudly.

Mark jabbed Craig painfully in the side with his elbow, fearing he might tell all. "We jumped him, and he ran away," Mark filled in.

The brothers helped their mother up slowly and into a chair at the table. She wrapped the blanket closely about her. "Would one of you get me a glass of water, please?"

Craig set the water in front of her. "You boys are my heroes," she said— and she meant it. "Can you do one more thing for me?"

"What's that, Mom? Anything," Mark responded.

"Your Dad doesn't know I feed the hoboes. Please promise me you won't ever tell him—or anyone—anything about this." The boys exchanged a quick glance. "And *don't worry*—I won't be feeding them any more after this."

"Sure, Mom," the boys chimed in unison, trying not to betray the relief they felt.

"This will always be our secret." And with that she enfolded her young sons lovingly in her embrace.

The brothers' eyes met, confirming their silent vow.

Mark, who was always conscious of the time, suddenly said, "My gosh, we'd better get back to school!"

"Oh, my goodness, yes! You mustn't be late. We might have to explain it to Dad. Hurry!"

Mark was already at the door, but Craig was savoring a last hug.

"Craig, *come on!*" Mark yelled, and Vicky reluctantly released her little boy.

3

Vicky sighed. Recovering slightly from her ordeal, she silently berated herself for going against her better judgment and letting hoboes into her home. She had always been afraid of them, but felt sorry for them at the same time. *Well, now I've learned my lesson—I was lucky this time, thanks to the boys coming home when they did. Never again.*

Getting to her feet, she looked around the kitchen to make sure all was in order. In the far corner, behind the door, a bright orange object caught her eye. She stooped for a closer look and saw a small piece of wood. It looked like a piece from the business end of a croquet mallet. She picked it up, and with a sudden start, dropped it as if stung: it was covered with blood!

Mind racing, Vicky stared at the blood on her fingers. She opened the back porch door, and sure enough—one mallet was missing: the orange one!

My God, I wonder if—those poor boys! she thought.

Then, remembering the pact with her sons, she disposed of the evidence and silently vowed never to ask them more.

. . . . .

They exploded from the driveway onto Water Street. Mark's heavy Schwinn gripped the pavement; Craig slid sideways. "Hey, what about lunch?" Craig yelled.

"Too late now!"

No time for more talking. Every effort was now directed at getting to school on time—all previous records fell. The bell rang as they flew across the school grounds into the bike rack.

"We'll bury him tonight," Mark said breathlessly, as they raced for their classrooms.

. . . . .

School was out for the weekend and Mark found Craig waiting

18

impatiently, already having mounted his bicycle. But this time they were in no hurry to get home. In the familiar surroundings of school that afternoon, what they had done became an unreal memory. But now, once again they came face to face with harsh reality.

"Where we gonna bury him?" Craig asked.

"Down in the woods," was Mark's answer. "Where else?"

Down in the woods! How often they had used that familiar phrase, always conjuring up visions of the glorious forest playground that swept from their backyard steeply down to the lake below. But now it took on a sinister new meaning.

Reluctantly, they slowly pedaled homeward.

Craig's face contorted, threatening tears. "I wonder how Mom is."

"We'll soon see," Mark said, picking up speed. "Remember, not a word to anyone about this—not even Karl and Meg," he added, thinking that their older brother and sister might already be home.

"I know, stupid! We promised Mom." Craig didn't dare speak that way to his older brother under normal circumstances—but this wasn't normal! And sure enough, Mark let it pass, since he had more important things on his mind.

They pulled into the driveway. There in the garage was the 1949 beige Plymouth.

"Geez! Dad's home already!" Craig said.

Quickly they wheeled back onto Water Street and cruised down the block. They knew they weren't ready to face Dad yet.

"Criminy! This is the weekend we were going down the bay!" For some reason, they had always said "down the bay."

"Wow, great! I forgot!" Craig answered excitedly.

"You stoop! We can't go!" Mark reminded him. "We have to bury him tonight!"

"Why does it have to be tonight?" Craig asked, having never missed an opportunity to visit the family cabin on Sunrise Beach.

"We can't leave him in The Playhouse 'til Sunday night, stupid. He'll start smelling, or someone might find him, or something. Anyway, this is our chance, while they're gone," Mark reasoned.

Craig looked crestfallen. "But we always go! How'll we get out of it?"

"Lemme think." Neither Mark nor Craig could remember a time they had not been overjoyed to accompany their parents on an outing to the bayplace. No simple excuse would do; this would have to be convincing.

Craig's face lit up. "Wait a second! Karl said we could go with him to the Puyallup Fair tomorrow if we wanted, remember?" Craig said.

"Oh yaaah! All we need to do is tell Mom and Dad we've decided to go to the fair with Karl. Let's go back," said Mark as he made a U-turn.

The brothers had learned to keep silent during their father's frequent tirades and avoided confrontation with him whenever possible. Many times they had been the innocent victims of his vicious attacks, and they were never allowed to defend themselves. "Don't talk back!" he would scream as he wound up to hit them whenever they opened their mouths in self-defense. So they had learned not to. It was with trepidation that they approached home now, since they had committed a deed that could not even compare to the trivial things that had brought such severe punishment down on them in the past.

Craig spoke Mark's thoughts. "Let's hope Mom hasn't said anything."

From the voices they heard, they could tell their parents were in the kitchen. They detoured around the house, entered through the sunroom door, and hurried down the steps to their basement bedroom. Since one of their father's outbursts could be generated when the boys were slow to change out of their school clothes, and wanting to play it safe this time, they quickly changed. "Let's go up," Mark announced soberly.

4

The night was dark with no moon. It seemed even darker under the thick canopy of trees deep in the woods. A single flashlight with weakening batteries provided their only light. Eerie shadows played about them. Mark and Craig were already hard at work digging.

Getting out of going down the bay had been easy. It seems Meg also had other plans—to stay overnight at her girlfriend's house. Their mother had winked and given their father a look that the boys secretly understood, and then she had said in mock pity, "Well, honey, I guess we'll be all alone." He had grinned widely, and it was settled.

The real problem had been brother Karl, whose room was at the back of the house overlooking The Playhouse. Since it was Friday, he was up late reading. He was always curious about his younger brothers' doings, and would be bound to investigate if he heard anything. Mark and Craig had agreed it was best that they wait until well after Karl went to bed.

His light finally went out about 1:00 A.M., and the boys laid low for an hour or so before they made their move.

The familiarity of the daytime woods was gone. Night had transformed them into a strange and fearful place. Unknown sounds came from out of the blackness all around them. Trying their best to put their fear aside, they concentrated on the task before them.

"What's that?" Craig cried with a sudden jerk. Mark jumped, causing him to dump his shovelful of dirt on Craig.

"You stupid idiot! Just shut up and dig." Mark didn't want to admit it, but he was just as nervous as his little brother.

They were down only about two feet when Craig said, "Isn't this deep enough?"

"Good grief, Craig!" Mark admonished. "They dig 'em six feet deep in the cemetery!"

"My gosh, that's over our heads! How we gonna do it?"

"Maybe we'll go less. I don't know. We don't want anyone to find him, so the deeper the better." Mark was figuring it out as he went.

At first, they had made slow progress, breaking through the surface layer of roots. The moist soil was tightly packed and heavy to shovel aside. Now the going was easier. The soil had become dry and sandy, and lighter in weight. Still, it was exhausting work. The hours of exertion dragged on.

Finally, Mark dropped his shovel and said, "That ought to do it! I couldn't lift another shovelful if I had to."

Craig, who hadn't been shoveling much lately anyway, collapsed in relief. "Let's go get him," he sighed.

The rope swing, dangling from a limb far above, cast a weird shadow as they climbed up the steep hill to The Playhouse. What they had to do next filled them with dread. Mark's hand trembled as he reached for the door; Craig had a tight grip on his big brother's belt.

What if he isn't dead after all? What if he's looking at us? What if he comes to when we're dragging him down the hill?

Mustering courage from somewhere, Mark opened the door. The hobo's lifeless eyes shone in the flashlight beam, vacantly staring upward. "C'mon!" he whispered. "It'll be light soon."

The Playhouse door faced the house. The body had to be dragged out and around to the top of the hill. They were in danger of being discovered by Karl, a light sleeper, until they were safely over the crest of the hill.

They had dragged the hobo into The Playhouse feet first, so they now had to reposition the body to drag him out the same way. They had not imagined that this would be so difficult.

"He's all stiff," Craig said. He was so stiff, in fact, that it was like trying to turn a solid plank around in a confined space. To make matters worse, The Playhouse was full of old lumber and discarded furniture.

"Rigor mortis," Mark coolly informed him.

"Huh?"

"Grab his ankles. I'll try to pull him around by his arm," Mark said. A cold chill crept up his spine as he tried not to think about coming into contact with the dead man. "Remember, we can't make any noise!"

Mark tugged at the hobo's left arm while Craig struggled with his feet. They were making headway when one foot slipped from Craig's grasp, knocking a loose board to the floor with a bang. The boys froze.

"Now we've had it! If you woke up Karl—" Mark whispered. He opened

The Playhouse door a crack and peered toward Karl's room for a long time. No light came on! "We were lucky this time. No more noise!"

Completing the turn, Mark moved to join Craig at the hobo's feet, and they slowly opened the door again. "One, two, three, heave!" Mark whispered hoarsely. The body began to slide through the door, then stopped.

"He's stuck!" Craig reported.

"It's his arm," said Mark. "It's sticking straight out. We have to get it down to his side." He grimaced. This meant they had to climb over the hobo back into The Playhouse.

"You go," Craig insisted.

"Chicken!" Mark cleared the hobo easily and landed inside. "You push and I'll pull."

They managed to budge the body back into The Playhouse a little. "Maybe that's enough," Mark said. "Lemme see."

Fiercely Mark yanked at the arm, knowing delay at this point meant certain discovery. Stiffened tendons popped as he moved the arm over and down. "There! I did it," he grunted. He rejoined Craig outside.

The hardest part seemed to be over, as they pulled the hobo easily across the dewy grass. Without hesitation they began their descent.

Then Craig lost his footing, and the dead man slid down into them. Suddenly they were tumbling head over heels—the brothers and their lifeless cargo—and they landed in a tangle at the foot of the hill. The dropped flashlight dimly illuminated the macabre scene. Mark opened his eyes and looked straight into the corpse's icy stare. He shrieked and frantically scrambled to free himself. Craig had one of the dead man's huge hands over his face and was immobilized with terror. Mark grabbed Craig's arm and pulled him free. Out of breath, hearts in their throats, they fell back onto a soft layer of ferns. Both boys shook uncontrollably. Finally, they looked at each other. They both knew there was no turning back now.

Slowly, hesitatingly, Mark got to his feet, and Craig followed. Without words they took up their burden once more. By a lucky accident, they had come to rest only a short distance from the freshly dug grave. Soon they had him on the edge, and they rolled him in with little effort. Both watched as the body landed face down in the hole, relieved that they had seen the last of those terrible eyes.

"All right, let's *bury* the sucker!" said Mark, releasing his pent-up rage. He was back in control.

The words seemed to spark new fire in them, and they began to furiously backfill the grave. The last traces of the hobo disappeared under a deluge of dirt. They had not even noticed the faint glimmer of first light touching the treetops above them.

Progress was swift. As the dirt approached the top of the grave, Mark stopped.

"Wait, Craig! We have to tamp down the dirt so we can get more in!" They dropped their shovels and leapt on the grave with a vengeance.

Having thrown the excess dirt into the bushes and covered the grave with brush and ferns, they took a last look around. They were satisfied that no one would ever know their secret.

· · · · ·

At last falling exhausted into their beds, they hoped for a little sleep. *No rest for the weary,* they had often heard their mother say. For the first time, it hit home.

"Hey, you little hanyaks!" came the call from big brother Karl. "Time to go to the fair!"

PART II

The sweet aroma of nearby gardenia blossoms blended with the more distant ginger that floated across Kalihiwai Ridge on the evening breeze. Mark drained the last of his brandy and reached for the bottle, savoring the scented air.

"You know, Craig, I still remember every detail. I feel the mallet snap in my hands. I hear the sound it made when it crushed his skull. How about you?"

"I can still see his eyes. After—what is it now—forty-eight years?"

"I remember you were haunted by those eyes for years."

The brothers talked on quietly for a time. They could not recall when they had last broached the subject of the hobo.

At length Craig bent down to the cardboard box, and reaching in blindly, withdrew his arm again. Dangling from a ribbon in his fingers was a heavy gold pendant. He held it up in the fading light so Mark could see.

"It's Dad's Medal of Honor, Mark!"

"Well, I'll be damned! Why in God's name would he pack *that* away?" Mark took the medal from Craig. "This explains why we haven't seen it in half a century."

"He never displayed it, that's for sure. Probably because of Ab. I'm sure you haven't forgotten The War Story, have you?"

"How could I?" Mark sighed. "Dad told it every chance he had—minus certain unknown details, of course!"

Ray's missing details were now well documented.

1

Lt. Raymond Buling Mosier cut a dashing figure in a naval officer's uniform. Of medium height and wiry build, he moved with the self-assured confidence of an athlete. He had been Pacific Coast collegiate wrestling champion. Women were invariably attracted by his blend of charismatic charm, humorous nature, and boyish good looks. Add to this his striking blue eyes and the golden voice of a crooner, and his exploits with the ladies had become legendary.

After the Japanese attack on Pearl Harbor, Ray had been faced with the toughest decision of his life. Supporting Vicky and their four children took all his energies, yet he felt the need to defend—with his life if necessary—the freedoms they enjoyed. He was torn apart by his own family, some taking one side, some the other. His mother was adamant that his place was at home; she heaped guilt on him, continually reminding him that he was safe from the draft. Others, eligible for the draft, including the cousins he had grown up with, were evading it.

Two things finally tipped the scales. One was his miserable job with a pipsqueak egomaniac for a boss; the other—the true deciding factor—was Vicky's heartfelt encouragement to do what she knew he had to do.

Ray had applied for and received a direct commission as full lieutenant in the U.S. Navy. This was a limited program whereby only a few exceptional men, meeting stringent qualifications including age, experience, and educational background, were accepted directly into active service without prior military training.

Two days after receiving his commission, Ray was proudly parading around showing off his new uniform in front of the family, when his orders arrived. Ray anxiously tore open the envelope.

"Listen to this, honey!" he boomed. "They want me to report to Great Lakes in two weeks! I'll be a battalion commander!"

"Isn't that nice," Vicky lilted, trying to sound happy. The realization hit her squarely that she was losing her husband—for how long she could not know.

. . . . .

Great Lakes Naval Training Center was a sprawling mass of long, khaki-painted barracks and staging areas on the shores of Lake Michigan at North Chicago. As Ray's taxi drove across the base, the tarmac was abuzz with activity: marching columns of men, olive drab trucks in caravans, thousands upon thousands of America's finest young men being readied for war.

Ray, believing in his own uniqueness, was making a quick ego adjustment to the amount of gold braid that he saw all around him. He wouldn't have thought it possible that the entire navy could have that much brass!

A chill wind blew in off the choppy waters of the lake and struck Ray full in the face as he climbed out of the cab. He paid off the driver, grabbed his seabag, and headed up the stairs of Command Headquarters.

The cabbie called after him. "Give 'em hell, sir! I'd be goin' myself, 'cept I got a wife and kids at home." Ray was already weary of hearing that excuse, which never failed to bring back feelings of uncertainty about what he had done, along with pangs of loneliness for the family he had left behind.

"Lt. Raymond Mosier reporting as ordered, sir!" He stood at attention and handed his orders across the desk to the commanding officer.

"At ease, son," the older man said warmly. "Is it Raymond?"

"Most people call me Ray, sir," he answered, his pent-up tension dissipating at the C.O.'s informal and cordial manner.

"Ray it is, then!" the captain responded, with a friendly smile. Ray could see already that he would get on fine with his senior officer.

"Let's see here. Ah, yes, you'll be commanding the Second Battalion, Ray," the C.O. said as he leafed through the orders. "Your exec has already reported aboard. I'll have the yeoman call him over, and he'll show you the ropes. Welcome aboard, Lt. Mosier! I'm looking forward to having you in my command. Let me know if there's anything I can do to help you out. You have direct access to me at all times."

"Thank you, sir!"

"Now, how about a coffee while we wait? You can tell me a bit about yourself. Yeoman!"

They were finishing their second cup of coffee when a rap came at the door, and the yeoman stuck his head in.

"Ensign Normal is here, sir," he reported.

"Send him on in!" the C.O. ordered.

The door opened wide and in walked a large, heavy-set man in a baggy, rumpled uniform, with a disheveled head of hair and at least two day's growth of whiskers.

"I see you dressed for the occasion, John!" chuckled the captain good-naturedly. "Meet your boss: Ray Mosier, John Normal."

As the two men shook hands, they appraised each other carefully.

Boy, I don't know about this guy, Ray thought. He couldn't imagine how anyone this unkempt could possibly command the respect of several hundred men.

Boy, I don't know about this guy, John thought. *Spit-and-polish for sure, by-the-book, no doubt a real bastard to work for.*

"Glad to meet you, John! Maybe you can give me some tips on proper dress code." Ray followed the captain's humorous lead.

John tightened his grip on Ray's hand, eyes twinkling, and let out a spontaneous guffaw. "You're gonna be all right, Lieutenant Mosier, *sir!*" He snapped to, and clicked his heels together for emphasis.

Perhaps, for all appearances, the two men weren't so different from one another.

2

Having been dismissed by the C.O., John led Ray to a battered Jeep parked in front of headquarters.

"This is your battalion vehicle, Lieutenant," John said, hoisting Ray's heavy seabag.

"It's elegant," he said facetiously. "By the way, John, I don't know what protocol is—but why don't you just call me Ray when we're not around the men?"

"Aye, aye, sir! I mean, Ray!" The twinkle was back in John's eyes. "Thought we'd head over to the BOQ first and get your gear stowed. I already got you a room assignment. Then I'll take you over to the battalion and introduce you to the troops. After that the rest of the day is ours."

"Sounds fine to me. I'm looking forward to you showing me around. Might that include a tour of Chicago's night spots?"

John was elated. This was a man after his own heart. There might not be a single barkeep—or gorgeous female—in all of Chicago who didn't know him by name and reputation.

"You're talkin' to the right man! Let's get duty out of the way and take this town by the tail!" John hoped that didn't sound too irreverent.

Many drinks and four nightclubs later, they arrived at the Ambassador East Pumproom in downtown Chicago. They entered the large, dimly lit room through a curtain of blue cigarette smoke, abruptly immersed in the din of the crowd, trying to spot a free table. Each man had acquired a beautiful companion—Ray thought it had been their second club where two of the loveliest ladies to walk the face of the earth had approached their table and greeted John intimately. Sally, a tall, lissome brunette, attached herself to John, and poor, defenseless Ray was left with Bridget, a statuesque blonde of unsurpassed beauty. It seemed to Ray that he and Bridget must be the only people in the whole place who weren't smoking.

This was all new to Ray. The farm boy, raised far from cities, had only dreamed that such things existed. Also, he was deeply in love with his wife, and never had looked at another woman. Yet, he was having no inner conflict, for he had entered a different world, a world where Vicky and the kids didn't exist, except as an abstraction. His marriage—he perceived—was safe at home.

The deep-seated feeling of the young men going to war—and their women—was quite fatalistic at that time. Most thought they'd never come home again; no one knew what tomorrow would bring. Ray knew if he ever did come home, it would be to his wife and family.

But for the present, he was the absolute captive of his fantasy. And he was going to go after it with great gusto.

The pert cocktail waitress, bustling in her little satin skirt, approached their table.

"Well, hi there, Ab! How's my favorite customer?" She raised her voice to be heard above the live band nearby. "What can I get you folks tonight?"

She took orders all around. As she sashayed off, Ray leaned toward John, who was lighting yet another cigarette.

"Say, John! What's this 'Ab' shit?"

John, nodding sideways at Sally with a sour expression, growled, "That's exactly what it is—shit!"

"He doesn't really like it," Sally explained. "It's because of the crazy things he does when he gets a little drunk. You know, with a name like 'Normal,' I guess it was just natural for people to start calling him 'Ab-Normal'! Now it's just plain ol' 'Ab.'"

"Correction. I never get drunk—I get happy!" John said. Ray couldn't tell whether or not his heavily slurred speech was deliberate. "It ain't normal to be called abnormal," John grumbled.

"Well, I like it—suits you like your uniform, John! From now on, it's Ab!" Ray laughed.

The band was playing a familiar tune, and Ray began to hum along. Bridget heard him and leaned closer.

"Oooh! You have quite a voice—sounds like Bing Crosby's! Listen everybody!" she said to their companions.

Ray, feeling good enough by now, let loose a refrain to the delight of his company. He felt Bridget's warm hand glide softly, unerringly, up his inner thigh.

"Gee, Ray, good looking and a golden voice, too?" Sally gushed. "Hey—

they just love it when they can get a customer—one who can sing—up on stage to croon with the band! Wanna give it a try?" And with that, she stood up and shouted to the band leader.

Next thing he knew, Ray was standing behind the microphone, facing the noisy, inattentive crowd. Although nervous at the prospect, he did love to sing and was secretly thrilled to have this opportunity. The band leader was looking at him quizzically.

"Do you know 'As Time Goes By'?" Ray asked.

"Does the navy have ships?" the band leader grinned, and launched into the prelude.

The hubbub died as the first mellow tones reached out to the audience.

> You must remember this:
> A kiss is just a kiss,
> A sigh is just a sigh!
> No matter what the future brings,
> As time goes by...

People looked up to see who was singing. From here and there throughout the club came shushing sounds as folks tried to quiet the more boisterous patrons. Soon, all eyes were riveted centerstage. The entire place was in rapt attention, listening in wonder to the unknown troubadour making his debut.

"He can have me!" swooned Bridget, her lovely face cradled dreamily in her palms.

"Me, too!" Sally agreed, sighing wistfully.

"Wait a damn minute! What about me?" Ab protested.

"Shut up and listen!" Sally chided.

As the last notes of Ray's vibrato faded into the night, not a sound could be heard for an interminable moment.

Oh God, I bombed, Ray thought despairingly.

Then, from somewhere in the back, it started. Slowly, tentatively at first, the applause spread. In seconds, the clapping and yelling swelled to a crescendo, and then people were jumping to their feet, cheering wildly, and the place was in pandemonium.

At Ray's table, not another drink had to be paid for that night.

3

The two men worked well as a team on the job, and off duty they became virtually inseparable drinking buddies. The months passed, and they had fallen into a routine of hitting the night spots every Wednesday and Saturday night, the best live-band nights—and thus the nights with the most action. Ray's growing notoriety assured them an abundance of wine, women, and song.

This particular Wednesday, though, Ray was a bit down in the mouth. Ab had just informed him that something had come up, and he couldn't make it tonight. Ray hadn't yet gone into Chicago without his chum, and wasn't sure he wanted to. He wondered what in the world would ever keep Ab from going along. Could it be because Ray had stolen the limelight?

Ray had knocked off for the day and was in his quarters thinking these thoughts as a tap came at his door. It was Ab.

"Well, if it isn't my sometime friend who's deserting me in my time of need! Or are you comin' after all?"

"Sorry to disappoint you, buddy. But I might be able to get away sooner than I thought and join you downtown later. Do you think I can trust you with both dames?"

Ray liked that proposition, and he made up his mind to go. "You drive a hard bargain, fella!"

"Wonder if I might ask you a little favor. Can you drop me off in Evanston on your way down? I got a couple errands to run, and I'll catch a cab from there."

Ray dropped Ab at a corner in downtown Evanston and pulled the Jeep back onto Sheridan Road heading south. He didn't see the black limousine slide up to the curb behind him. Nor did he see the door opening to swallow his friend into the dark interior.

The big black car made a turn toward the lakefront and soon entered an area of dilapidated, mostly abandoned warehouses. As it approached one of these, large bay doors swung slowly open, the car disappeared within, and the doors closed. In the dim light Ab could just make out a dark figure, sihouetted against a naked bulb on the wall behind him.

Clutching the fat manila envelope he had brought with him, Ab stepped out of the vehicle and approached the solitary figure. The man extended his hand to receive the package, which Ab surrendered without ceremony, then quickly turned to leave.

"Heil Hitler!" The exploding words echoed off the walls through the hollow shell of a building.

Ab wheeled around again to see the shadowy figure, right arm thrust out stiffly toward him, frozen in the familiar Nazi salute.

Clicking his heels smartly, Ab returned the salute.

"Heil Hitler!" he erupted proudly.

4

Following their eighteen months of duty at Great Lakes, the two men had not surprisingly received orders to the same operation: the Naval Armed Guard, based in New York City. Their excellent teamwork had earned them a place on the same convoy as their first assignment.

The Naval Armed Guard was an unheralded part of the navy's wartime operations. There just weren't enough warships to protect all the convoys crossing the North Atlantic. So usually several merchant ships in each convoy were outfitted with woefully inadequate armament that might include a 4-inch gun mount on the forecastle. A fortunate few also had as many as eight 30-caliber machine guns mounted to port and starboard. Small contingents of naval personnel, with a junior officer in charge, were then assigned to each of these vessels to man the guns. These ships would be stationed on the perimeter of the convoy to protect against German attack from above or below. It was a pitiful effort at best, for when under attack they were always outmanned and outgunned. Seldom were they successful in preventing sinkings.

It was to two of these hapless contingents that Lt. Ray Mosier and the newly promoted Lt. (j.g.) John Normal had found themselves assigned as Armed Guard Commanders. Further, being the "Senior Officer Present Afloat," Ray had been assigned the dubious responsibility of "Convoy Armed Guard Commander," an officious title that carried little authority.

Now it was April 1944. Ray and Ab sat drinking at the Copacabana. They had run into each other at their favorite Manhattan watering hole a couple of hours ago and had discovered that they were both between convoys, awaiting assignment. They had not crossed with the same convoy since that first one a year ago, although each was now the battle-scarred veteran of six round trips to England. Ab's convoys had lost three times the tonnage suffered by those Ray had commanded. At the moment, Ab was engaged in bragging to Ray about the vast superiority of his combat experience.

"Three times the tonnage means three times the amount of guncrew excellence," Ab muttered.

"Excellence my ass! It means the Krauts sank three times as much, which means my gunner's mates are three times better than yours! It just makes me wonder what the hell you'd do if you were on the run to Murmansk!"

Ray, of course, had no way of knowing that these statistics were the direct result of his best chum's espionage. Ab had been feeding his Nazi counterparts secret information on the exact movements of the convoys to which he was assigned. On any given day, the precise location of every ship in Ab's convoy was known to the enemy. On each crossing, the ship to which Ab was assigned was identified on all enemy charts with a large red "X," which meant "verboten"—"hands off!"

5

"I just got off the phone with Ed Teller, gentlemen," President Roosevelt was saying. "He assures me the bomb will be ready for delivery within two months."

The small group gathered together in the Oval Office included the Secretary of State, the secretary of the navy, the secretary of war, and of course Harry Hopkins, the president's closest confidant. The nation now had the means to bring the war to a quick conclusion, and these powerful men were meeting to finalize the plan for the European theater.

The president continued. "Way I see it, all we need to decide is the best way to deliver our proposal expeditiously to the Russian underground."

Besides the bomb, one of the best-kept secrets of the war was the existence of a well-financed, well-organized, well-directed Russian underground. Powerful figures in the top levels of government and military—particularly the Red Army—were committed. The sole mission was the overthrow of Stalin and the Communist regime.

And this movement had the full support of the United States and its European Allies.

"Suggestions, gentlemen?"

The first to speak was Frank Knox, SecNav. "By your leave, Mr. President. We've got it all worked out. With your approval, we can get the wheels rolling right away." He looked from man to man and received a nod from each.

"Let's hear it," Roosevelt said.

"Right, sir. In six weeks one of their top operatives will be in Murmansk. We already have a convoy scheduled to make the North Russia Run in that time frame. The tricky part was finding the right individual to be our courier—and we've found him."

"And who might that be?" Roosevelt prompted.

"Lt. Raymond Mosier, USNR, sir," Knox continued. "He's our top Armed Guard commander. He's commanded half a dozen North Atlantic convoys and has lost less tonnage than any of our other commanders. He's a real fighter, sir!"

"Tell me more. Can we trust him?" the president asked soberly.

"Absolutely. He left a wife and four kids to serve his country, and by all accounts, he's incorruptible—not a blemish anywhere on his record. One of the true patriots, I'd say, Mr. President."

"I assume that you gentlemen are all in agreement?" Roosevelt looked at each man in turn, and each response was the same.

"Yes sir, Mr. President!"

"Good. Let's go with it, then. Only two more quick items, then I'll let you go. Henry?" he asked his secretary of war.

"Sir?"

"I'd like you to summarize the message for the present company, to make sure we're all in full agreement."

Stimson straightened himself in his chair and began. "The message will of course be in code, in fact four of our newly developed codes. We do not believe the enemy can possibly decipher them. It'll read something like this: 'The bomb is ready. We now have the means to immediately end the war. Simultaneous with our destruction of Germany, we will have the ability to drive her remaining forces from your borders. Concurrent with the surrender, you must begin your revolt against Stalin. All other specifics are in place and remain as previously agreed to. We await your agreement to initial target Hamburg and date August 1.' That's about it, sir," Stimson concluded.

"Good. Short and to the point. Everyone in agreement?"

The grave silence in the room confirmed that they were.

"Just one more thing, then. Cord?" He addressed the secretary of state, Cordell Hull.

"Sir?"

"Can you confirm for this group that the Allies are with us on this?"

"Yes, sir. All on board, anxious to get this thing over with. Of course, the Brits want to drop the first one!"

"Well, maybe they should get first crack. Let's think about it. That about wraps it up, gentlemen, unless you have anything further."

As the men rose to leave the Oval Office, Roosevelt called out a last command.

"Oh, Frank! Get Lieutenant—is it Ray?—Mosier down here to see me right away. I want to personally hand him the package."

"Aye aye, sir! I'll get right on it."

. . . . .

Ray was reading the terse cable for at least the seventh time as the train sped through the darkness toward the nation's capitol:

U R G E N TU R G E N T***U R G E N T***
PROCEED SOONEST VIA SURFACE TRANSPORTATION
TO WASHINGTON DC STOP ADVISE ARRIVAL PLACE
AND TIME STOP LOOK FOR NAVY VEHICLE STOP
YOUR PRESENCE REQUIRED AT PENTAGON
MEETING STOP RETURN HOME PORT 24 HOURS
END

It was as much of a mystery as the first time he had read it. The message gave no clues about the purpose of the meeting, who else would be there, or why Ray was included. *Oh, well,* Ray thought, tiring of the mental strain. *One thing I know how to do is follow orders!*

Ray had never been to Washington before, so he had the driver giving him a commentary as they passed various notable landmarks.

"There's the Pentagon!" he noted as the car whizzed past.

The vast building slid from view before Ray, momentarily overwhelmed, realized what had happened.

"Wait a second! My meeting's at the Pentagon!" he exclaimed.

The driver glanced around in surprise. "Sir, my orders are to deliver you to the White House!"

Ray was stupefied by this pronouncement.

"Are—are you sure you've got the right man?"

"Lt. Raymond Mosier, right, sir?"

As he was ushered into the Oval Office, it occurred to Ray that his knees hadn't been this rubbery since he faced the Pacific Coast wrestling champion back in his college days. He was meeting with the President of the United States!

As the door closed behind him, he realized he was to be alone—completely alone—with his commander in chief, Franklin Delano Roosevelt.

What in the hell do I do now? he thought foolishly, coming to full attention, hat properly tucked under his left arm. *Should I salute?* Protocol wasn't his strong suit anyway, and he definitely wasn't prepared for *this* situation. But he needn't have worried.

"At ease, Ray. Have a seat. This is going to be just an informal chat."

Ray gratefully eased into the waiting chair opposite the president, who sat behind an enormous desk—in a wheelchair. Just in time, for he felt in another moment his legs might have given out.

"Ray, my staff tells me you're among our best fighting men—a man we can trust implicitly. Would you say that's a fair assessment?"

"Wow, sir—uh, Mr. President!" were the first immortal words Ray would utter to his Chief.

What do I say next? he thought stupidly. By now the adrenalin was flowing, and he was regaining self-composure.

"I don't know how to judge about the fighting part, but I love my country, and if that means trust, you can trust me with anything, sir!"

The president squinted, assessing the man carefully. His spectacles glinted, and the long cigarette holder arched upward between his teeth, revealed now in a broad grin—vintage FDR.

"You're our man, all right! Listen closely, son, because this is the only time you're going to hear this."

Incredulous, Ray listened intently to what followed.

"We've got a message for you to deliver to a contact in Murmansk. Have you been to Murmansk?" Roosevelt knew he hadn't.

"No, sir, but it sounds like I'll be going there soon!"

"*Very* soon!" the president chuckled. "Your convoy leaves New York next week for the North Russia Run—better known as the Run to Murmansk. You should have your orders to that convoy by the time you get back. The crossing takes twenty-two days on average, and you'll be contacted on arrival there." He reached into a drawer of his desk and withdrew a heavy gold cigarette case, which he handed across to Ray.

"No, thank you, sir. I don't smoke."

"That's gratifying. But that's not what I'm giving you." The president paused to emphasize the gravity of the pronouncement that followed.

"What's in this little case may very well determine the future of the world!"

Ray caught his breath. After a moment, he answered, "And—that's what I'm to deliver to Murmansk, sir?"

"That's it, m'boy! It's locked tight, and the key's at the other end of your trip. And believe me, you don't want to know what's inside anyway!"

"No, sir!" Ray bellowed with renewed vigor.

"I don't need to tell you, Ray, there's only one destination for this package. And that's the one I've already told you about."

Ray pondered this for a moment. "What if the worst happens, and I'm captured, Mr. President?"

"Deep-six it. And quick. Except for that, never let it out of your sight. It must not—it *cannot*—fall into enemy hands. Any more questions?"

"I understand, sir. You can count on me. Thank you for your confidence. I won't let you down, Mr. President!"

"That's it then, Ray. Good luck and Godspeed!"

Ray knew their meeting was at an end, for the president had already bent to other tasks.

6

"Well, ol' chum, my orders came today! Look's like my number's finally come up. I'm off to Murmansk next Monday," Ray was saying to Ab as they sat at their regular table at the Copacabana. This time the two were alone and the drinks were flowing freely. And this time, Ray was matching his friend drink for drink, as if there were no tomorrow.

"I'll drink to that, you poor bastard!" Ab slurred, as he raised his glass in mock salute—he knew this was also known as the "suicide run," and that far more tonnage was sunk on the dreaded Murmansk Run than on any other North Atlantic crossing.

Ray was fairly bursting at the seams to tell Ab the rest of the story. The foggy state of his mind made clear thinking difficult. He could think of no valid reason to keep it from his trusted friend. *The president didn't tell me not to. And after all, this is my best chum,* Ray reasoned with himself. *Ah well, why not?*

"You ain't heard nothin' yet," he announced, pulling the shiny gold case from an inside pocket.

"What's this? Don't tell me you started smoking!" Ab said, expecting Ray to open the case.

"Nope. Must admit I was fooled too, when the president handed it to me." He tapped the case emphatically. His besotted words were indistinct, but dead serious: "Herein lies the future of the world!"

To a sober observer, the change in Ab's demeanor would have been dramatic. He sat bolt upright, eyes clear and wide, now showing no signs of inebriation.

"Whoa, buddy! President? You met the president? Future of the world? Slow down, you're way ahead of me!" The sudden clarity of Ab's speech went unnoticed by Ray.

Ray launched into a detailed recounting of his meeting at the White House. Ab was dumbfounded by what he heard, his mind racing. *How can I get my hands on that message—without Ray finding me out? Damned if I know—but one thing's for sure: I've gotta be on that same convoy!*

When Ray finished, Ab once again affected the slurry speech he had so quickly dropped moments ago. "Hey, Ray ol' chum!" he began. "I've heard Russian pussy is the best there is! And how the hell do you expect to find any without the best pussy-chaser this side of the Atlantic?" Then, a bit more gravity in his voice: "Seriously, buddy, I'd give my eye teeth to be with you on this one! I'm still waitin' for an assignment—can you pull any strings?"

"Are you kiddin'? It's wide open! Never would have thought to ask you—figgered there's no way you'd want the Murmansk Run. You got yourself a job!"

"Lt. Ab-Normal reportin' for duty, sir!" He threw Ray a sloppy, decidedly non-reg salute.

The two men laughed loudly, drained their drinks, and proceeded to close the place down.

. . . . .

Ray was meticulous about his job. Part of his responsibility was to inspect each ship under his command prior to departure of the convoy. This convoy was a large one, made up of sixty-seven ships, to be accompanied by only eight Armed Guard vessels. Ray was now boarding the ship he had assigned to his friend Ab, really pleased to have not only a close chum, but— he thought—a very proficient naval officer, assisting him on this dangerous mission.

The two men completed their inspection of the eight-man gun crew and their weapons, and Ab turned to his senior officer.

"Got a couple minutes, boss? I'd like to show you my quarters. I got a little surprise for you," he added with a wink.

"Sure, why not? This is my last inspection, and anyway I want to make sure you're not ridin' in the lap of luxury!"

Ab was definitely settled in. His cabin was awash in paraphernalia, rumpled uniforms lying here and there, the deck covered with debris, the entire place in disarray. Ab reached into a small safe mounted in his stateroom desk and produced a bottle.

"How 'bout a drink, partner?" he said, with another wink.

"Ab, you know that's against navy regs—you better get rid of that right away. We really gotta be on the bit this time." Ray was back in his command role, with a vengeance.

"You're right—aye, aye, sir!" Ab snapped, putting the whiskey back where it came from. The sound of the bottle making contact with a metal object attracted Ray's attention. He bent to look into the safe's interior.

"What's that you have in there?" he asked curiously.

"A couple souvenirs I got from Germany, before the war. Oughta really be worth something when this is all over," he said, withdrawing what looked like a tin can on a stick.

"A hand grenade!" Ray exclaimed, accepting it gingerly. "Is it live?"

"You bet your sweet ass! And if you've heard about these Kraut grenades, you'll know they're unpredictable as hell. They've been known to blow in as few as two seconds—and as many as twelve—from the time the pin is pulled. And do they pack a wallop—about twice as big as ours!"

Ray wolf-whistled. "What I wouldn't give to have one of these babies!"

"Well, I got two here. What am I offered for one?" Ab joked.

"What do you want?"

Ab reached back into the safe and retrieved the bottle, cradling it against his chest. "*This* baby is all I want!"

Ray was silent for a long moment. "You got yourself a deal, my man. Just tell me you'll go easy on it."

"My word is my bond. The grenade's yours! Remember what I told you, though—handle it with kid gloves."

Ray gripped his prize tightly and left the cabin. As the hatch clanged shut behind him, Ab popped the cork and took a long, deep draft. "Plenty more where *this* came from," he uttered through a stifled laugh that caused whiskey to escape from one side of his mouth and run down his chin in a trickle.

7

Seventeen days out the attack came. At least a dozen Messerschmitts roared out of the gray early morning sky, guns blazing mercilessly. A wolf pack of U-boats attacked simultaneously, and three torpedoed ships were exploding, smoking, breaking up, going down.

Ray's feet hit the deck, and he had his crew at general quarters within seconds. No sooner were the men on station than a low-flying fighter strafed the deck, and three of his crew lay dead or dying before firing a single shot. One of the casualties was his veteran 4-inch gunner, the only one qualified, besides Ray, to operate this gun. Ray instinctively climbed behind the long barrel and took over.

"Load 'er up!" he yelled to his ammo handlers as he swung the mount into action. Framing his first aerial target in the crosshairs, he commenced firing without hesitation.

Results were immediate. His very first shot produced a plume of black smoke that signaled a direct hit. He watched in awe as the wounded Messerschmitt exploded into the ocean close aboard.

Not far to port, on the nearest Armed Guard vessel, John Normal lay still in his bunk, dead to the world, in a drunken stupor. His guns lay silent, with no one to command them to action.

Ray was having a heyday, firing at his first live enemy. It seemed he couldn't miss! A second enemy aircraft was aflame and burst apart in midair. Pieces of the destroyed fighter rattled onto the deck around them.

The third attacker was on him before his men could reload. A sudden, stunning impact knocked him from his perch, and he found himself, dazed, flat on his back on the deck. One of his men ran up and bent over him.

"Sir! Are you hit?" he cried.

"I—I dunno—it's my chest! Feels like I got hit by a cannon!" His fingers probed for what he feared must be a terrible, gaping wound. As he was withdrawing his hand, it struck something hard in his breast pocket. A flash of recognition crossed his mind, and he extracted the gold cigarette case.

Dead center was a quarter-inch-deep cavity, the unmistakable imprint of an enemy projectile.

My God, it saved my life! he thought, quickly slipping it back into his pocket.

"I'm all right!" he gasped, letting the seaman help him to his feet. "Let's get back at it!"

Ab was still unconscious. The sounds of battle began to stir some vestige of awareness. One of his crew was futilely hammering on his locked cabin door. His guns remained ominously silent. Strangely, his ship had not been attacked.

As Ray painfully regained his perch, one of his men called out.

"Mr. Mosier, look!"

He looked to starboard and saw the telltale wake of a torpedo speeding directly toward the ship.

"Brace yourselves, men! It's gonna hit us amidships!"

They held their breath for the explosion, as the wake disappeared beneath their ship. Nothing. *Maybe it's a dud,* Ray thought.

The next voice was that of the port lookout.

"Sir, look at this! It must have passed under us. There it goes!"

They rushed to the port side. They thought they caught a glimpse of the rapidly receding torpedo heading away from them. Ray lifted his eyes to follow its trajectory.

It was moving in a direct line toward the ship on his port beam. *Ab's ship!* he thought in horror. He watched as the projectile unerringly closed on its unintended target. As it disappeared in silence, Ray thought hopefully that it might have missed a second time.

A gigantic explosion dashed his hopes, as the torpedo struck just aft of amidships. A quick succession of blasts confirmed that the hit was a bull's-eye, as the boilers and munitions blew skyward. Ray was transfixed as he watched his friend's ship break in two and begin to go down, his knuckles white where he gripped the railing.

It was pandemonium on Ab's ship. Men were tripping over each other, falling and jumping over the sides. No one took charge. Ab finally stumbled to his feet, his survival instinct pulling him out of the depths. He yanked the cabin hatch open, tripped onto the wildly tilting deck, and fell overboard into the icy waters of the North Atlantic.

"Lieutenant!" Ray's starboard lookout shouted. "There's the U-boat—I can see it! It's at periscope depth!"

Vengeance burning in his soul, Ray jumped back onto the 4-incher and brought it to bear on the enemy sub.

"Keep me loaded, men! I'm gonna get those bastards!"

Over the next few minutes he furiously pumped shells at the sub, lowering and elevating the gun to perfect his range, sweeping the boat from stem to stern. The U-boat came about and pointed its bow at Ray's ship, making itself a smaller target, and released its last two torpedoes.

As the black obelisks slid menacingly toward them, Ray saw that the sub was surfacing. At that moment he saw the unmistakable glint of an oil slick spreading out from the wounded sub: he had scored a direct hit!

"You got 'er, sir!" the men cheered as the U-boat rolled onto its side, settling quickly into the depths whence it came.

Their elation was short-lived. The ship was rocked by one thunderous concussion, followed immediately by a second as the missiles made contact. One of them ignited the magazine, and the other struck the engine room. The ship was a blazing inferno.

Since the guns were of no use without ammo, Ray went down on deck to cast loose lifeboats and direct the abandoning of the doomed ship. He was all too aware of the hazards presented by the arctic conditions at these latitudes, so after loading the last lifeboat, decks already awash, Ray rushed into his nearby cabin and donned his rubber lifesaving suit. He looked around, hurriedly checking to see if there was anything worth saving. He spotted his prized possession: the German grenade. He tucked it inside the rubber suit, zipping it over the bulging object with some difficulty, and headed back on deck.

Ray darted here and there, dodging the intense flames, fearing further explosions, searching for any stragglers or injured crewmembers. He was on the fantail when the deck fell away beneath him, and he found himself floundering madly to escape the strong downward suction created by the swiftly sinking hulk that had been his ship. As soon as he was free of this undertow, he looked around for a lifeboat. He heard men screaming and turned to see one lifeboat caught in a huge whirlpool, spinning crazily and getting sucked down into the vortex. For a few seconds it looked as if it would go under, but suddenly it was flung free, and as chance would have it, it floated toward Ray. One of the men recognized their commander.

"Lt. Mosier! Over here, sir!" he yelled excitedly. The others in the lifeboat reacted quickly and paddled toward their leader. Soon Ray was being pulled aboard the half-full lifeboat.

"Did everyone make it?" was his first thought.

"Yessir, every man still breathin'," was the answer.

Glancing at the ample space in the boat, Ray recalled that Ab's ship had gone down close aboard and gave the order to search for survivors.

The men had renewed confidence, drawing strength from Ray's calm and determined leadership. After what he'd done to save them, they'd follow him into the fires of hell!

Many men were floating here and there, widely separated by the turbulent seas. Ray was directing the grisly rescue effort. Many of the bobbing figures were corpses, either dead from wounds or from exposure to the frigid elements. Without a rubber suit, a man wouldn't last more than fifteen minutes in these waters.

Ray had almost given up hope of finding Ab alive when, incredibly, he thought he heard singing—someone was singing—in a slurry, hoarse voice. He spotted a two-man raft that resembled an oversize donut. The singing seemed to be coming from the raft.

> Rub-a-dub-dub,
> Three men in a tub
> Lost on the ocean blue—
> I'll roll like a hub,
> Sing rub-a-dub-dub,
> 'Cause you broke my heart in two!

Ray smiled broadly. He knew that voice—and it could only belong to one person.

"Ab! You sonofabitch! Living up to your name, I see!" he cried gleefully. "Get his big worthless ass in here, men. Meet Lt. Ab-Normal! We can make room for one more, can't we?" he said, noting that the lifeboat had now far exceeded its capacity.

"Huh?" Ab looked around, barely comprehending his surroundings. It was later rumored that the high level of alcohol in his blood was what had saved him from certain death from hypothermia.

As they pulled the drunken man over the side, one of Ray's men couldn't resist bragging about his boss.

"Guess what, Mr. Normal? Commander Mosier sank a U-boat—and downed two Kraut fighters, too! How'd you do?"

"Huh?" was still the only response Ab could muster.

"Doubt he even had time to think—remember, he got hit by that first torpedo that went under us," Ray reminded the man, as he attached a line to the donut raft, so it would float alongside.

There were many heads still visible bobbing on the sea, so Ray had the men turn the lifeboat away and they commenced to search for additional boats and rafts with room to pick them up. They had reached a point perhaps a hundred yards from the nearest survivor when the rushing sound of displaced volumes of water behind them caused all heads to turn.

A U-boat was surfacing close abreast of the remaining survivors, positioned such that the lifeboat was aft of its starboard quarter—on its blind side. The decks were still awash when they heard the clang of the conning tower hatch, and a man quickly emerged, climbed down from the tower, and proceeded toward the bow on the catwalk, still nearly awash. Dumbfounded, the occupants of the nearby lifeboat watched as the man prepared the forward machine gun and commenced firing at the hapless survivors floating off its port side.

Instinctively, thinking of his 45-caliber sidearm, Ray gestured at his men to approach the sub. *This is a long shot,* he thought. *But it's worth a try!*

Ray's oarsmen dug deep. The gap was narrowed: 75 yards, 50 yards, 25 yards—and they were close aboard, just aft of amidships to starboard. The gunner was firing to port, proficiently executing his victims. Ray was hoping to get a clean shot without ever being seen. As Ray unholstered the pistol, some sixth sense must have alerted the machine-gunner, for he turned and spotted the lifeboat. He reacted instantly, and began to swing his mount in a 180-degree arc to take a bead.

Ray steadied himself. He raised his weapon, releasing the safety, and took careful aim. He emptied the clip as he found himself looking into the barrel of the machine gun. The man jerked back involuntarily as the bullets ripped into him. His lifeless body careened wildly off the narrow deck and disappeared over the side. Not a shot had been fired in their direction.

As Ray was firing, he felt the straining bulge beneath his tight suit. An idea was forming in his mind. *The grenade!* he thought. *I wonder—!*

Heads were already appearing in the conning tower, and he knew he had to act now, or they'd all be fish-food. He unzipped his rubber suit and withdrew Ab's gift, gripping it tightly by its long handle. *I may have only two seconds,* he thought, recalling his friend's warning.

Ab was finally coming out of his fog. Ray's gun had gone off right in his ear, and he was jolted back to his senses. The events replayed themselves rapidfire as he surveyed the remnants of the convoy receding in the distance. Closer in was the resounding evidence that the intelligence he had transmitted to the Nazis had been put to good use. The smoldering remains of the disastrous attack were all around him. *They must have sunk at least twenty ships,* he gloated.

But then it dawned on him. *The assholes targeted my ship!* Ab could see the futility of his present situation. The Germans wouldn't know he was among the survivors on this lifeboat—he might have been one of those helpless men floating out there! He fumed at the thought. Then he saw Ray fumbling with the grenade, and knew what he had to do.

"Hold on there, boss! You don't get all the glory today. Only one U-boat per man!"

Before Ray could stop him, Ab tore the grenade from his grasp, pulled the pin, and lobbed it into the conning tower, where it fell unerringly through the open hatch below the feet of the startled Germans. There was a mad scramble of confusion aboard the sub.

Ab was shouting at the top of his lungs. "Get this goddamn rowboat outta here! She's gonna blow!"

The lifeboat was gaining momentum, heading away from the sub. Ab and Ray were positioned in the stern, closest to the sub, when they heard a muffled WHUMP! reverberating from its interior.

Ray, standing to get a better view of the U-boat, noted that it appeared to be intact.

"Uh-oh! Doesn't look like *that* could've done much damage!"

And it wouldn't have, had it not ignited the sub's munitions.

No sooner had he uttered the last word than the enemy vessel literally lifted into the air and erupted in an immense geyser of water, oil, and metal. The resulting concussion was the largest explosion any of the men had yet experienced. They were too close to escape unscathed. Concurrent with the horrendous, ear-shattering roar of the blast, the full force of the shock wave hit the two officers—who were both standing in the stern—and blew them into the air like rag dolls.

Ray sputtered to the surface amidst a burning oil slick, finding himself treading water for the second time in the same day. He had no time to think. He took a deep, foul breath of the black, smoky air and submerged again, swimming frantically to escape the burning surface. As he began his underwater breaststroke, the movement sent daggers of blinding pain through his right shoulder. The excruciating throbs threatened unconsciousness— only the icy water kept him going. He swam until he felt his lungs would burst, and surfaced, choking and gasping, only to find himself still surrounded by smoke and flames. *One more dive ought to do it,* he assured himself, taking another deep breath and going down.

This time when he surfaced, he was beyond the flaming slick. The agony of his pain caused him involuntarily to reach for his shoulder. His fingers came in contact with the ragged edges of a gaping wound. Looking down, he saw that he was bleeding heavily. *Must have taken a shitload of shrapnel,* he groaned. *Gotta find that lifeboat or I'm a goner!*

Barely managing to keep his head above water, he scanned the horizon in all directions. He could see no sign of life—no ships, no planes, no subs, no lifeboats.

The skies were darkening, the seas were building, and the winds were rising. One of the frequent, deadly North Atlantic storms was on its way.

Ray felt the last of his strength ebbing away. He was continually slipping beneath the waves, unable to make the effort to stay afloat. He floated in his mind to a warm, comfortable place: he was with Vicky, who tenderly cradled his head in her lap, and reassured him softly, lovingly, that everything was going to be all right.

Several hundred yards away, Ab had managed to escape the flaming circle. As he surfaced, he couldn't believe his dumb luck. Not more than a hundred feet away was the donut raft, with a lone occupant.

"Over here!" he hollered, waving madly with one arm while struggling to stay afloat. As the raft approached, the man recognized him.

"Mr. Normal! Is that you?" He was incredulous. "Are you all right?"

Ab's heart sank as he recognized one of the gunners from his own ship.

As he pulled Ab aboard, the man launched his barrage. "What happened to you back there? Why didn't you man the guns when the ship was attacked? We never had a chance! She went down with all hands—you and I gotta be the only ones left!"

Ab was fully aboard the raft now. Slowly, deliberately, he reached to his hip, drew his .45, aimed it squarely between the man's widening eyes, and pulled the trigger.

"Now *I'm* the only one left," he said with evil satisfaction.

. . . . .

The hallucination shattered as Ray was shocked back to painful reality. Something had ahold of him, was pulling on him—hurting him. It pulled him spluttering to the surface.

"Does this mean I get another medal, boss?"

Ray thought he must still be dreaming. *Wasn't that Ab's voice?* he thought through a bleary wall of pain.

Sure enough, he recognized his friend's oil-blackened face, just now contorted with the strain of snatching Ray from the icy fingers of doom.

"Lucky for both of us I found my little dinghy!" Ab exclaimed. Ray was too far gone to notice that Ab had somehow reclaimed the two-man donut raft. The pain and exhaustion overwhelmed him, and with a groan he faded into unconsciousness.

Ab noticed the blood pulsing from his friend's shoulder. On closer inspection, he found a sharp piece of metal protruding from the wound. His first-aid training told him he had to do two things—and fast: remove the foreign object, and stop the bleeding.

Having no tools, Ab gripped the slippery fragment delicately between his thumb and forefinger and ever-so-gently worked it loose. He removed it proudly and thought, *A piece of a U-boat—that I sank!—a better souvenir than a grenade any day!*

He searched the interior of the raft, and besides the canvas bailer, he found some oil-stained rags. They would have to suffice for tourniquet and bandage.

Soon, Ab had the wound wrapped and the flow of blood was down to a trickle. He looked around to survey the situation.

There was no one in sight to rescue them; no food or water to sustain them; and a monster storm was a-brewing. *Other than that, everything's hunky-dory!* he laughed to himself. It was so hopeless, it was funny.

By nighttime the storm had reached its full fury. Ab was forced to bail continuously to prevent being swamped by the mountainous seas. The frigid wind penetrated to his very bones. His hands and feet were numb from the ever-present, unavoidable icy waters. He knew this was going to be a long, sleepless night. He almost envied Ray, protected by his rubber suit, lying there in what looked like a peaceful slumber.

Sometime after midnight, during a brief lull in the storm, Ab found a moment to rest from his frantic activity. As his mind drifted here and there, the words came back to him out of nowhere. *'The future of the world!' My God, the secret message! I wonder if he's got it on him!*

He feverishly began patting Ray's inert torso and almost immediately located the object of his search. He unzipped the rubber suit far enough to reach into the inside pocket and withdrew the damaged case. He held it in his two uncontrollably shaking hands. Without warning, it popped open.

I'll be goddamned! It's sprung!

He could discern nothing of the contents inside the case. He would have to wait until daylight and hope that Ray did not come to before then and find it missing. He slid the warped piece of gold into his own pocket and wearily resumed his bailing.

Ab was a well-trained Nazi counterintelligence officer and was blessed with a photographic memory. As the first weak rays of stormy morning light reached the small raft, he withdrew his prize and made quick work of its coded contents. He carefully returned the parchment to its container, snapped it shut with difficulty, and gingerly replaced it in Ray's pocket, zipping the rubber suit safely over it. *Wonder what the hell it says!* he thought, curiosity burning within him. *I bet Hitler would give his last remaining testicle to get his hands on this!*

Returning to his tiresome task, he began to review the incredible events of the previous day. His own ship had been lost—sunk despite its *verboten* designation—while he lay in a drunken stupor, not a shot having been fired in its defense. His one hope was that there were indeed no more surviving witnesses to his inaction. The counterfeit story of his personal heroism to save his ship was forming in his mind.

Dead men tell no tales, he thought.

· · · · ·

Ab had passed out from sheer exhaustion. He now jerked awake from his fitful slumber and was amazed to see that the storm had passed. The transformation was spectacular: the sun was up in a blue sky, the sea was like glass, and the last of the storm clouds were roiling off over the distant horizon.

Ray's pasty-white complexion prompted Ab to check on his friend's condition. His pulse was weak but steady, and his breathing was regular. He sat back, thinking about their slim chances of getting picked up.

He was pessimistically searching the horizon. He blinked at something—a spot in his eye?—but it remained: a black dot, right where the sea and sky met. *It couldn't be!* he thought. *A straggler?*

The convoy was no doubt far ahead of them by now, so their only hope might be a straggler—a ship that had fallen behind the rest—purposely to avoid attack, or because of engine problems, or simply because it couldn't maintain the convoy speed.

Ab's mind was racing. He knew this would be their only chance at survival. The odds were overwhelmingly against being spotted by a lone ship at sea. Many factors were involved, not the least of which was lady luck—and he had already had more than his share of that! Calm seas were a must. But the determining factor would be the proximity of the passing vessel to the tiny raft. Ab was painfully aware that he was without flares.

He noted with rising hope that the liberty ship seemed to be on a direct course for them! Still, he knew that the ship would have to pass close aboard for them to be spotted. He remembered his sidearm, and realized that the loud report would carry far across these placid waters. He waited until what he determined was the closest point of approach, then emptied the clip into the air.

There was a momentary lull. Then there came a shrill series of whistle blasts—six short hoots—which Ab recognized as the international distress signal. As he watched, the ship veered sharply and pointed its bow head-on toward the raft and its two occupants. In minutes, the SS *Gravenstein* pulled alongside and a rope ladder was lowered.

Safely aboard, Ray had regained consciousness after his wound was sutured and properly dressed. The corpsman had removed two additional pieces of shrapnel with his forceps.

No one noticed the tiny pin-prick above his throbbing right temple.

Both men had been fed and clothed. Ray had found his precious cigarette case still in the pocket of his ruined uniform on the chair beside his bunk, and had discreetly transferred it to his newly acquired khakis.

The *Gravenstein* had been zigzagging in search of the two officers. Its crew had earlier rescued the other lifeboat survivors who had witnessed the dramatic sinking of the U-boat.

Tales of the two officers' daring exploits were rampant throughout the ship for the remainder of the Run to Murmansk.

8

The docks at Murmansk could berth only about a dozen ships at one time, but the port had many good anchorages. It was to one of these that the *Gravenstein* found itself assigned.

As it appeared there would be some delay in off-loading their cargo, Ray called a meeting of the convoy's surviving Armed Guard commanders and ships' masters. The purpose was to assess losses and damages so that he could report to the naval attaché at the U.S. Embassy. The results of the attack were calamitous: 19 ships lost, 20 damaged, 92 men dead or missing and another 141 injured. Injuries ranged from bad to awful, with Ray's lying somewhere in between—he suffered from terrible daggers of pain piercing through his shoulder and arm, as well as increasingly severe headaches. But he had escaped infection, and thanks to Ab's prompt ministration to his wound, he was healing quickly. As he left the meeting, he stopped to chat with his friend.

"Hey, ol' chum! Been meaning to tell you, I aim to recommend you for the Big One!" he confided.

"The big what?" Ab quipped.

"The Medal of Honor, you dumb asshole!" Ray expostulated.

Ab, absorbing the full irony of this revelation, gloated inwardly. To Ray, he presented a look of amazement, then offered his hand.

"I'm gonna see what I can do about you too, boss!" Ab promised.

"I'm on my way to make my report at the embassy. I'll see what I can find out about the nightlife in this godforsaken place, and let you know when I get back."

"Like I said, Russki pussy's supposed to be the best!"

. . . . .

Ray entered a spacious lobby with a large reception desk at its center. Behind it sat a middle-aged wisp of a woman wearing horn-rimmed glasses. Ray presented his credentials to her.

"Oh, yes, Lt. Mosier! We've been expecting you! We heard about the awful attack. I can't tell you how happy we are to see that you made it through that ordeal!" She was genuinely sympathetic. "Please follow me, sir," she said, leading him down a long corridor to an interior room of the embassy. "The naval attaché will be right with you."

The door closed behind her, but within minutes it swung open again, and in walked a navy commander.

"Lt. Mosier—thank God you made it! I'm Commander Whitfield," the senior officer said warmly, extending his hand. "Guess you've got the bad news for me, eh?"

"Yessir, and I'm afraid that's just what it is!" he answered, handing over his report.

"Have a seat while I look this over, Lieutenant."

Ray accepted graciously; his shoulder bothered him considerably, and the headache was coming on again. He waited in silence until the commander spoke.

The man rubbed his eyes wearily and tossed the report on the desk, shaking his head. "These damn convoys'll be the death of me yet!" he cursed. "First things first though, Lieutenant. Did you make it through with the package?"

"What package might that be, sir?" was Ray's impassive response.

"The gold cigarette case that FDR handed you personally!"

"Oh, yes sir! I managed to hold onto it, but it did take a direct hit from a Messerschmitt machine gun!"

With a relieved expression, Cdr. Whitfield reached into a pocket and withdrew a snapshot, which he handed across to Ray.

"This is your contact. Memorize the face, and the name on the back. For obvious reasons, I can't let you keep it."

Looking out at Ray, black eyes blazing, was a dark-haired Russian beauty. The aristocratic structure of her face was accentuated by high cheekbones and full, sensuous lips. Ray was entranced. He turned the photo over and read aloud:

"'Tatiana Nobolokov'—did I get that right, Commander?"

"That's close enough. Think you can spot her?"

"No problem, sir!" Ray said enthusiastically.

"The Soviets are pretty strict about fraternizing with their girls. In order to keep the trouble down, they've set up some clubs where the foreigners can dance—and that's all!—with carefully selected young ladies of 'impeccable conduct' sent up from Moscow. Most of them work as interpreters during the day, so they're fluent in English. You're to meet Tatiana at the Red Star Club at 2100 hours tomorrow to make the transfer."

"Aye aye, sir! And thanks! My next question was going to be about the nightlife here, and you've already answered it!"

. . . . .

Ab wound the requisitioned Jeep through the drab, narrow streets of downtown Murmansk as Raÿ kept a lookout for the Red Star. The city and its port, which lay only thirty-five miles from enemy airfields, were under almost constant aerial attack, so a total blackout was enforced. Without the precise directions given him by the commander, Ray wouldn't have had a prayer of finding the club. The commander had humorously told him the story of the giant neon star atop the club, dwarfing it, that in peacetime lit up half the city with its red glow. But now, it was visible only during the day.

"Thar she blows, Ab!" Ray announced. "Right where Whitfield said it'd be! Let's park this baby!"

They were met at the door by a massive, sour-faced peasant woman, attired in nondescript pseudo-military garb. She frowned at them disapprovingly, but allowed them entry.

The din was reminiscent of clubs back in the States. The place was elbow-to-elbow with people, apparently gathered in the most popular—or only—night spot in Murmansk. Ray thought that the acrid clouds of smoke were the worst in his experience, and as he coughed spasmodically, he felt the first twinges of an oncoming headache.

"It's that Russian tobacco, Ray! You all right, chum?" Ab asked.

"Unfortunately, I'll probably live," said Ray facetiously.

Ray wondered how he would ever make contact with Tatiana in this mass of humanity. *There must be three or four hundred people here,* he thought helplessly. The raucous sounds of amateurish music reached their ears from the far side of the room.

"Sonofabitch, if it isn't live music!" Ab joked. "I better grab me one of these lovelies before they're all gone. Catch up with you later, buddy!"

That was the last time Ray ever saw Lt. (j.g.) John Normal.

. . . . .

60

The evening wore on. Ray danced with a bevy of stunning Russian girls, but so far none could challenge the girl in the photograph. He still sought Tatiana.

He should have known that she would find him. He turned to leave the floor following a dance, and she glided into his arms as the band began to play a Russian waltz.

"It's my favorite!" Her melodic words came softly, almost in a whisper, yet emphatically clear. "I think I've found my man."

Ray looked into those incredible eyes and was lost.

"Hello, Tatiana."

She was exactly his height, and he was immersed in the wondrous scent of her. Suddenly her presence, there in his embrace, was all that mattered. No one else existed. They drifted together in a dream over the dance floor.

Tatiana's lips gently brushed his ear as she whispered, "I have a flat nearby!"

"But they told me you can't leave!"

"We have a saying in Russian: 'Sneaky mouse escapes hungry pussycat.'"

"That's good enough for me!" Ray laughed. "Let's get outta here!"

As they approached the door, the stone-faced matron suddenly presented a toothless smile, winking fondly at Tatiana. She hurried to open the door, and the couple slipped silently into the night.

Tatiana gripped Ray's arm tightly and led him down the black, unseen streets as confidently as if it were daylight. Ray was totally in her hands, but he knew instinctively that he could trust her. There was a flight of stairs, Tatiana fumbling at the lock, and then they were inside. She produced a match from somewhere and soon a kerosene lamp glowed dimly in the stark interior.

Her passion seethed. Clothes were a cumbersome barrier and could not be cast off soon enough. She stepped out of her dress and threw herself upon him hungrily, pulling him with her onto the small divan. The heat of her body was like an elixir and he felt himself melting into oneness with her. Suddenly she broke free of his embrace, and he felt the fire of her lips exploring his body. His throbbing vitals oozed in anticipation. She knew he was ready and sensuously rolled over, offering him the wonders that lay within her, opening herself to him. As he slipped into her, he thought he would swoon from the warmth coming from her loins into his as together they approached the threshold of fulfillment.

Several hours later, the flame of their lust subsiding, they lay lazily entwined on the disheveled divan.

"Say, handsome stranger! Didn't you have something to give me?" Tatiana asked playfully.

"I gave you everything I had, baby!" Ray laughed. "Unless of course you want your package wrapped in gold," he added sarcastically, as he reached for his discarded jacket on the floor beside him.

They made love again and again. When they parted late that night, Tatiana made it clear they could not risk another liaison. Ray had fleetingly hoped for a longer affair with his Russian lover. But the farewell had in it all the fateful suggestions of finality.

An exhausted Ray Mosier dragged himself from his bunk the next morning and staggered to the galley for coffee. His head was pulsating with pain, but nonetheless he sought out Ab, anxious to tell him about his wild night and to see how his friend had fared. Surely not as well as Ray had!

Ab wasn't in his bunk. Ray went up on deck and asked the watch if his friend had been seen.

"Lt. Normal hasn't reported aboard, sir. But I have a message here for the two of you. It's from the embassy."

Ray read the handwritten message:

Lt. Mosier and Lt. (j.g.) Normal:
Please report to me at the Embassy
at your earliest convenience.
Respectfully,
Robert Whitfield, CDR USN

The *Gravenstein* was anchored well out on the perimeter of the convoy, so Ray had the coxswain come close aboard ships that were en route to the shore. He would call out to ask if any of the Armed Guard crews had seen or heard from Lt. Normal since the night before at the Red Star. Since all replies were in the negative, he proceeded ashore with growing concern.

Ray was standing alone before Cdr. Whitfield. "Lt. Mosier reporting as ordered, sir!"

"I have *two* important messages for you, Ray. That's why I wanted to deliver them personally. But—where's Lt. Normal?"

"He appears to be missing, sir. I just discovered he never came back aboard ship last night. Last time I saw him was at the Red Star."

"Happens all the time. Probably sleeping it off somewhere. Well, this concerns him, too, so you can pass it on when you find him. First, your convoy gets underway for the States *tomorrow* at 0600!"

"Wonderful, sir!" This was unbelievable. Ray knew that some convoys were delayed in Murmansk for months. "That means I don't have much time to look for Ab—uh, Mr. Normal."

"We'll see what we can do to help. Second, based on all the glowing reports from your men, I've made a determination that both you and Lt. Normal are deserving of our nation's highest commendation. I am in the process of preparing a citation recommending the two of you for the Congressional Medal of Honor!"

Ray's jaw dropped open. "Th—thank you, sir!" he stuttered, finally regaining his senses.

"It'll take several months, but I'm pretty damn sure these will get approved. I don't know anyone in this man's navy who sank a U-boat with a 4-inch shell, let alone a hand grenade! And the lives you saved by picking off that U-boat gunner—!"

"Thanks again, sir! If that's all, I'd better direct a search for my chum. If he doesn't turn up before we sail, can I count on you to keep an eye out and contact me when he's found?"

"Absolutely, Ray! I'll do everything I can."

. . . . .

The next morning, the convoy sailed without Ab.

PART III

The giant golden disk of the full moon rose above the shimmering Pacific, lending a soft glow to the lanai where the Mosier brothers were immersed in memories, oblivious of the glorious sight.

Mark was gazing at an old color photograph, hand-tinted in the style common in bygone days. Ray sat bare-chested on the shady lawn surrounded by his four rosy-cheeked children.

"Here's that portrait of us with Dad, taken in Portland during the war. You'd think we were the model family!" There was a faraway look in Mark's eyes.

Craig looked over his shoulder. "'The halcyon days of summer!'" It was a favorite saying of their father's.

"Yep, it was summer, all right. Look at our jumpsuits!"

"Hey, remember the kid with the suitcase, the day we left Portland?" Craig said suddenly.

"You mean Ralphie! He wanted to move away with us, and you told him he could!"

"Ralphie…I can still see him standing there…."

The brothers compared recollections but could come up with little else about Portland. Only that it marked the beginning, as far as they knew, of their father's severe reprisals.

Craig's crime had been chewing up a red crayon. Using soap, Ray had scrubbed his tongue until he gagged, then brushed his teeth until his gums bled.

Mark had broken the hall window. Ray had told the attending physician the broken glass had cut him.

1

In what was to be one of the last acts before his untimely death, Franklin Roosevelt had pinned the Medal of Honor on Lt. Mosier. It had been the high point of Ray's life, particularly when the president had gripped his hand, winked in recognition, and whispered confidentially, "I remember you, son—job well done!"

Only the absence of his good friend John Normal lessened the euphoria of the experience.

In addition to receiving the medal, Ray had been promoted to Lieutenant Commander and had been given a plum assignment as a result of his heroism in the North Atlantic. He was naval port director of Portland, Oregon, a position he held until the war ended in 1945.

· · · · ·

The naval housing project in Portland had been the Mosier home during this last year of the war. Now the war was over and it was being converted to civilian housing. Military families were given notice to vacate.

But they had a place to go. Vicky's spinster aunt had recently died and left her huge nineteenth-century Victorian home in Olympia to the Mosiers. This was Vicky's hometown, and Ray had also grown up in Washington State. They were happy to be returning to their roots, settling down after the many moves forced upon them by the war. And because of Ray's war record, he already had received some feelers from influential people in state government.

Of the four youngsters, only Karl and Meg really understood what was happening. Ten and eight respectively, they had been in more schools than they could count. They had learned to avoid making close friends, to spare themselves the agony of leaving them behind. Mark and Craig, not yet in school, had no such reservations. In fact, Craig had the perfect solution: he would just take his friend along with the family to their new home!

Ralphie stood on the sidewalk, dwarfed by the enormous suitcase at his side. The old Green Hornet was parked in the driveway. The trailer hitched to the car was overloaded with all the Mosier possessions. Mark and Craig were engaged in animated chatter with Ralphie.

"Let's go, you kids!" their father yelled.

All three headed for the back seat, Ralphie dragging the suitcase behind him.

Karl protested: "Daddy, they're bringing Ralphie!"

"Oh no, they're not!" Ray snorted. "Ralphie, go home!" The boy's face fell as he shrank back.

Vicky saw the boy's eyes welling with tears and went quickly, quietly to his side. In her unique way, she found words of comfort.

"Ralphie honey, we're going too far away for you to come with us. Your mommy and daddy need you and would miss you, so you have to stay and take care of them. Right now, I'll bet they wonder where you are."

He sniffed sadly. He started to trudge home as they backed onto the street, but then turned to watch as the car pulled out of sight. As Ralphie waved feebly, Craig and Mark felt the agony their older brother and sister had known. Ralphie disappeared from view—and from their lives—forever.

Ray continued down the street, testing the big old car's ability to handle its ungainly load. Soon he found the main highway leading north to their new home, and they were on their way.

2

Several weeks later, Mark and Craig were still exploring the wonders of their newfound world. The big old house sat well back from Water Street on a huge parcel of land that included the still unknown woods falling away to the lake below. Even though within sight of the stately dome of the capitol building a few blocks away, in many ways it was like living in the country.

The house itself was enthralling to the boys, only slowly unlocking the mysteries that lay within. The entire upstairs and a large apartment at the rear were off limits, as they were occupied by long-term tenants who came with the house. But the living space left to the Mosier family was more than enough to stir the imagination of two young boys.

From the street, the house loomed up massively, its imposing Victorian architecture giving the neighborhood a link with olden times. Even though painted a drab, dark brown color, its formidable presence would cause people to stop and stare. Towering above the many-gabled roof was the monumental brick chimney, higher than any around.

Approaching via the front walkway, one was struck by the wide expanse of the front porch. Broad wooden steps stretched along its full length. Two of the five outside entrances to the house were located here. The one on the right opened onto a stairway that led to the rented upper floor. The door on the left was the main entrance for the Mosiers, leading first into a "sunporch" that served as an office for Ray when he worked at home.

From the sunporch a glass-paned door on the right led into the large, comfortable living room, with its overstuffed furniture and ornate, floral-patterned carpeting. The most commanding feature of the living room was its great fireplace along the outside wall, constructed of fine, dark burgundy bricks. Vicky, an accomplished pianist, had placed her old upright piano against the inside wall, opposite the fireplace. This was her prized possession.

Immediately to the right were the double French doors opening into the parlor, with its large picture window overlooking the porch and flowering front lawn. This was presently serving as the master bedroom.

Proceeding through the living room, one passed into the dining room under an impressive, open archway flanked on both sides by deep, built-in bookcases. Almost filling the dining room was the gigantic antique table with its huge hand-carved legs. Along the wall to its right stood the substantial matching buffet, surmounted by an aging beveled mirror. In the nearside corner of the dining room was the old black telephone, sitting on its dainty triangular table, its dial displaying the four-digit number of the day. On the far side of the room a staircase wound its way up to a locked door leading to the rented floor above.

In the center of the left dining room wall was a hallway leading to the kitchen and other rooms in the rear of the house—that part of the house facing the enticing woods that lay beyond. The narrow, dark hallway was bordered on the left by the single bathroom in the Mosier-occupied portion of the house—with its ancient plumbing fixtures—and on the right by a tiny "sewing room" that served as Meg's bedroom. Meg's room was so small that the door would open only part way, where it was blocked by her little bed. On the rare sunny days, a few weak rays of light just managed to filter in through a single miniscule window located high up under the eaves.

Past the bathroom and Meg's room was the big, homey kitchen. The monitor-top refrigerator stood in the corner on the right, and just beyond it, under the back porch window, was the table where the children normally ate breakfast and lunch. The door leading onto the porch was just past the table. Windows on the rear wall overlooked the back apartment, the sweeping lawn and gardens, and the woods beyond.

On the left entering the kitchen was the sizable register, delivering heat from the forced-air oil furnace in the basement below. On a chilly morning it was common to find a dog, two cats, Mark, and Craig all crowded there together enjoying the toasty breezes. Next to the register was the electric range, which would add its warmth when in use.

In the center of the kitchen floor was the long, rectangular food preparation table, dubbed by the family the "tin table." Around the perimeter were spacious countertops, above which more than ample cupboards lined the walls, except where the oversized kitchen sink intruded. Above this was a window overlooking the capacious sunroom, with its stairway to the basement. In the far left corner of the kitchen, to the right of the sink, was the door that opened into the sunroom.

The sunroom ran perhaps half the length of the house, and had an outside entrance directly opposite the door from the kitchen. Another locked door led into the back apartment. Windows lined the outside wall of the sunroom, hence its name. Vicky used this as a utility room—washing clothes in the wringer washer, hanging them on clotheslines in the sunroom to dry when it was raining, which it often was; ironing; and sewing.

To the left of the kitchen door were twenty ugly concrete steps that led from the sunroom down to the dank, dark basement—known as "The Dungeon" to the boys.

Since bedrooms were in short supply, this was where the three brothers were fated to sleep. Little did they know it would be for seven years! The Dungeon's ceiling, walls and floor were bare, coal-blackened concrete. Thick, dust-laden cobwebs were everywhere. It would have been roomy but for the enormous furnace and its heating ducts that spread out like the tentacles of an octopus in all directions. Karl took over the far side of the furnace room. Mark and Craig were relegated to what once had been the coal storage bin, since converted to a tiny pantry, on the near side by the stairs. There was barely enough space for the bunk beds that had been obtained from war surplus, but the room was further crowded by miscellaneous paraphernalia their father had tossed in.

Worst of all was the fear Mark and Craig felt at night. They were afraid of the blackness that surrounded them, and the grimy cement floor was always damp and cold. They were isolated from their parents, who occupied the bedroom upstairs, all the way at the front of the house. If it hadn't been for Karl on the other side of the furnace, they would have been too terrified to sleep. By far the most fearsome, though, was the open crawlspace. It lay midway up the stairs, with its earthen floor reaching into oblivion under the recesses of the house. They felt that this was a corridor through which wild and unknown things of the night could reach out for them if they dared pass. It was no wonder that the brothers did not often venture out of their tiny room after bedtime.

Since the only bathroom required a trip up the stairs past this gaping menace, such trips were made only in times of greatest need. And, after their big scare, they were not made at all.

One night well after midnight, Craig just couldn't hold it anymore. He slowly crept out of the lower bunk, fumbled for his slippers, and then whispered vainly in an attempt to wake his older brother: "Mark!" He could not bear the thought of going up those stairs alone.

Mark was sound asleep, and even when Craig tried to shake the upper bunk, there was no response.

Shuddering, Craig made his way silently to the bottom of the stairs. One step at a time, keeping to the far side away from the crawlspace, he ascended. His eyes, trying to pierce the blackness, were just coming level with the dreaded opening. Once before, Mark had warned him not to look, but his fear drew him in. And there, shining from somewhere in the bowels deep under the house, were the eyes, watching him! He let out a spontaneous squeal, but stood riveted to the spot: the eyes had him transfixed.

He thought he would not ever move again when something bumped into him. He jumped and fell backward down the stairs, and the something was falling with him. As they landed, a dim light came on from the other side of the furnace. Karl looked down to see his two brothers writhing in terror on the cement floor. Craig recognized Mark and ceased his struggling.

"What in the world are you guys doing this time?" Karl demanded.

"Going to the bathroom," was Craig's pathetic reply. Obviously, he no longer needed to go.

After this, the empty fruit jars lining the pantry shelves found a new use; a lifetime later Karl would tease them about the urea crystals of many great and wondrous shapes they had grown in those unemptied jars!

3

Olympia was a small town, but it seemed boundless to young boys growing up there. They were familiar with only the parts within several blocks of their home, but what wonders were within their domain!

The expansive yard surrounding the house was of course most familiar of all. It was bounded on one side by a holly hedge, and scattered over the property were many additional holly trees. There was a birch, a hawthorn—and most important—a giant big-leaf maple tree waiting to be conquered. Flowers and flowering plants were everywhere: sky-blue hydrangeas on both sides of the front porch, ornamental begonias in a planter between them, showy rhododendrons growing on a trellis high as a house, sunny yellow buttercups around back, and the fragrant honeysuckle bush growing profusely up and over the back porch. There was a small garden encircled by the front walk brilliant with pansies, offering a colorful greeting to all who passed by. On one side of the entrance walkway, lovely lavender lilacs added to the delightful scene. Dainty, aromatic sweet peas climbed to the roof on the back of the garage. Also in the backyard was a "victory garden" dating from the end of the war, where the Mosiers grew every vegetable imaginable. Wild blackberries and raspberries were plentiful, and a cherry tree's branches offered tempting fruit within reach of The Playhouse roof.

The Playhouse; it was an odd name, because they seldom if ever played there. It was not a playhouse in the usual sense, since it had not been built for children. They had heard it was once used as a chicken coop, but it seemed too solidly built for that. Although it would have been ideal as a storage shed, not much was ever stored there. It might have made an excellent guest house if fixed up, but their father didn't have the time or inclination for that sort of thing. He may have known he'd never get around to doing anything with it when he told Mark and Craig it was theirs. So there it sat on the edge of the woods, largely neglected, awaiting its destiny.

Water Street was like a dream. It ran six blocks from the capitol buildings south to where it joined the street that led past the museum toward the grade school. It was a lazy, tree-lined street, with so little traffic that almost everyone who drove by was well known to the boys. Residents of the houses on the west side of the street benefitted from the wooded wonderland that stretched down to the lake below.

Change was almost nonexistent in those days. Up the broad sidewalks would come a handful of state workers at the end of the day, always the same, their routine unaltered for more years than anyone could remember. Each summer, they were the best customers at the Mosier boys' Kool-Aid stand.

Change also came slowly in the boys' lives. Mark started school in 1946, and this brought the biggest transformation, because the brothers were separated for the first time in their lives.

Mark's world now reached beyond Water Street—a full three blocks beyond! And he made new friends, some of whom lived in their own neighborhood. Mark now had an exciting new worldliness that set him apart; he seemed more distant to Craig, who suddenly found himself forced to play alone.

Craig's dilemma ended one year later when he too started school. Once again, the boys were inseparable, except when they went to their different classrooms. They shared the new experience of school, and they shared friends. Unlike many older brothers, Mark never excluded his little brother, and after awhile his friends became Craig's friends.

While school had expanded their boundaries outward, they had finally been awakened to the exciting frontier that lay down in the woods. Slowly, cautiously, over a great deal of time, they had begun to enter the fringes of this dark, mysterious, even foreboding place. Each foray took them a bit deeper, and with each venture the nearer parts became more familiar and made the woods seem less impenetrable. They bestowed names on their favorite places and features as they grew more comfortable in their new wooded realm. There was a stump shaped like a chair that became The Throne. Below this was a rectangular colonnade of trees enclosing what became The Room.

The woods became to the boys like a giant park that stretched off into an unknown wilderness, hidden away behind their own backyard. Each day after school they couldn't wait to revisit what they had found and to see what new adventures lay in store.

Now the full glory of their private paradise was unfolding to them. There were silent valleys, grassy meadows, and small streams. Common among the wildflowers carpeting the forest floor were trilliums, lifting their solitary blossoms, brightening the shadows. Ferns grew thickly, adding to the lush greenness, and leaves covered the ground like a wet blanket. Lilting birdsong echoed from the canopy above. Far down past the lowlands across the bogs lay enchanting Capitol Lake, drawing them ever nearer.

One day the boys learned to fly among the trees, and it was the height of their joy. Their father had tied a thick rope from the limb of a tree that hung high over the steep hill just below The Playhouse. At the lower end he had fashioned a large loop to allow the flyer to sit or stand as he soared out and away from the jumping-off place. The rope swing's notoriety spread quickly through the neighborhood, and their sanctuary was forever compromised.

Mark was the most accomplished on the swing, owing partly to his longer period of experience and partly to his superior body weight. By deftly shifting his torso in the loop, he had learned to swing ever higher, grazing the very treetops. On these flights he began to catch captivating glimpses of the lake flashing through the foliage. He mastered a technique whereby he could make the swing stall for a long moment, to prolong the view; then the slack would suddenly be taken up with a jerk, and he would plummet back toward earth, with the vision held firmly in his mind's eye. These visions he would recount to Craig, who had not yet been able to duplicate Mark's height on the swing and so had not seen the beckoning lake.

"It's really neat," Mark exclaimed, using their favorite word to describe wonderful things. "I can see the lake from up there, and I can stop the swing for a second to look."

"Wow!" said Craig with genuine admiration. "Wish I could."

"Maybe we could try it together sometime. You're probably just too little to go that high. But I'm telling you, there's something about that lake. We have to go find out sooner or later," Mark replied.

Craig was intrigued. The next chance he had, he convinced Mark to take him along on the rope swing. As they swung higher and higher, Craig suddenly cried, "There it is! I can see the lake!"

In both boy's minds, the lake became the final goal, the culmination of their childhood explorations. Therefore, its discovery had to be delayed so that they could savor the ultimate accomplishment. They did not talk about this; they just knew it to be true.

4

Craig sat in his second-grade classroom, his gaze fixed on the window. Huge, soft snowflakes were falling outside, sticking to the marbled glass and accumulating in the corners of the windowpanes. Craig watched as the snowflakes formed the perfect outline of a face—a man's face—and the snow encircled two dark spots that suddenly became a pair of sunken, vacant eyes—looking at him!

Already the playground was covered by several inches of snow. Craig could hear Miss Morgan droning on, her monotonous tone beginning to seem like part of a dream. Her voice was like a thread, barely connecting him to reality, but loosening its hold as the words she read faded into his fantasy.

Outside the wind howled out of the north. Temperatures plummeted to the teens, and skies darkened ominously. The full fury of the greatest blizzard in Olympia's history set in that winter morning of 1949. It hit so suddenly and with such force, there was no time to prepare. The day had begun so mildly, mothers had sent their small children to school without hats or mittens. And of course, blizzards were practically unheard of in the area, never known for having harsh winters. Lack of experience in dealing with such extremes in weather led the principal of Lincoln School to make an ill-timed decision.

"Craig—are you all right? You look like you've seen a ghost!" Miss Morgan was gently shaking Craig. "Come on, school's out! The principal says everyone can go home, but right away before the storm gets any worse!"

"Huh?" He returned from his dream to see that the class was in a turmoil. Gleeful boys and girls were crowding into the cloakroom, jostling one another as they grabbed their coats in an effort to be the first one outside.

"Wow! Neat!"

Craig had missed the principal's announcement, and now had to make up for lost time.

"Now, go straight home, children!" Miss Morgan advised. "No dilly-dallying!"

But Craig didn't hear. There was too much to experience. The feeling of catching snowflakes on his tongue. Pretending he was a pilot flying through Antarctica. Throwing snowballs at his retreating friends. And, he had to make some angels with his arms and legs, lying on his back in the fresh snow.

Craig was just admiring his finest-ever angel when Billy Stolski came along and trampled it, laughing maliciously.

"Hey! Quit it!" Craig yelled, without much authority.

"Who's gonna make me?" He tripped little Craig, and taking him by the scruff of the neck, painfully washed his face with snow. Satisfied, the bully went on his way.

This put an end to Craig's enthusiasm, and he set out dejectedly for home.

With great difficulty, he made his way down 21st Street to the Red & White Store on Capitol Way. There was no School Patrol to stop traffic on the normally busy thoroughfare, but there was no traffic to be seen.

Not that he could see very far; Craig's poor eyesight hadn't been improved by Billy's face-wash, and the snow blew straight at him. He may as well have been blind.

He cautiously stepped off the curb, but his feet slipped out from under him so fast that he couldn't break his fall. He landed flat on his back, and the back of his head cracked against the curb. He lay there trying to catch his breath, knowing he had to move before a car came along. He struggled to his hands and knees, head reeling, and scrambled across the icy pavement to the other side.

Completely disoriented and barely able to stand in the force of the gale, Craig began to inch his way in what he thought was the homeward direction. He had lost all feeling in his hands and feet; snow crystals clinging to his face created a mask of numbness. He continued on until the physical world faded once more, and reality became his dream. He settled comfortably into a soft snowbank.

Formed out of the white swirls, a large and familiar structure took shape before him. Bright sunshine warmed his shoulders, and the smell of springtime flowers was sweet in his nostrils. He was home, he was safe. The house on Water Street beckoned him in, shimmering its welcome. He happily drifted up the walk, entered the door, and floated into his bed. The blanket of snow drifting over his body became soft, warm, white sheets.

As Craig began to slip away, the friendly vision altered. He was outside again, looking in, and it had become very cold. The porch had become a wicked grin. The jutting roof was an ugly, hooked nose. Worst of all were the attic windows. These had become two vacant, terrible eyes, staring into his very soul.

Craig lay motionless as the snow piled atop him, covering him without a trace. Piercing winds howled down the empty street, driving the snow into ever-deeper drifts.

. . . . .

Mark bounded into the house. "Craig! Craig, you home?" he yelled.

Karl ran up, looking worried. "You mean he's not with you?"

"No—I thought he'd be here! I looked all over for him at school—second graders were already let out," Mark blurted.

"Those stupid hanyaks—what're they doing sending little kids out in this storm?" Karl said hotly.

Meg heard the commotion and joined them. "What's that? Craig—Craig's out there? C'mon, let's go look for him!"

"I'll write a note for Mom and Dad—in case they come home. Everybody get bundled up—let's get going!" Karl took charge.

"Look!" Meg said. "Tito wants to go!"

The dog was scratching and sniffing frantically at the front door. He was medium-sized, black with a white necktie, probably a Labrador mix. Though originally Meg's pet, he had claimed Craig as his own. Mark, equally attached to Tito, could tell that the animal knew something was amiss.

"We might end up losing him, too—that's a blizzard out there!" Karl warned them.

"C'mon, Karl! Tito might help us find Craig—you know how much he likes him," Mark coaxed.

Karl nodded in approval, and they pushed through the door, shocked by the suddenness of the icy wind whipping into them. "Stay together! We'll go up Water Street first," he commanded. Since sidewalks were covered in deep drifts of snow, he led the way down the middle of the street, retracing their normal route home from school.

Progress was painstakingly slow. The raging blizzard had become a monster threatening to consume them. One after the other would slip and fall, and regaining their feet took a colossal effort. Trial and error proved that linking arms was the best method to stay upright.

As they struggled up Water Street, Tito took an unexpected turn onto

19th Street, which was *not* the normal route to and from school. Mark tried to call him back, but their pet was soon lost in the wildly swirling snow.

"See, I told you—now we're gonna lose our dog!" Karl's shouted words were blasted away, unheard on the wind.

Mark changed direction to follow Tito, pulling Karl and Meg with him. Karl did not protest, knowing Mark and Craig each had an uncanny sense for the other's whereabouts.

Tito soon was faintly visible, probing the snow deeply with his muzzle, zigzagging from drift to drift. He turned briefly to acknowledge that his young masters were following his lead, punctuating the frigid air with a tremendous sneeze that sent a white cloud of frosted breath flying from his snout. He returned tirelessly to his search as the Mosier siblings followed, watching in fascination.

Tito caught the barest remnant of a familiar scent. He bolted to the side of the street, and began scratching furiously at the foot of a snowbank. Hearing his high-pitched yelps, the three jumped to the spot, scooping aside handfuls of the heavy snow. Karl uncovered something.

"Oh, God! It's Craig—it's his foot! Quick—he's buried in the snow! We have to get him out—c'mon Mark, here's his other foot! You grab it, and I'll pull on this one!" In order to be heard, Karl had to shout this right into Mark's ear.

In a matter of seconds, Craig's inert body was pulled free of the snowbank. Tito was licking the snow off his face. Meg was near hysteria as she observed her little brother's blue pallor.

"Is he alive?" she shrieked at Karl.

"He's—breathing, all right—but barely! Let's get him home and thaw him out!"

Karl and Mark hoisted Craig between them, and they turned into the teeth of the storm, moving toward home—the real home this time—at a snail's pace.

Desperate determination took hold of them as they finally entered the sanctuary of the big old house. Without words, they seemed to know instinctively what to do. Karl and Mark placed Craig on the sofa and lifted it over to the fireplace, where the fire Karl had lit earlier still burned. He piled on more wood until the flames blazed high up into the chimney. The two boys tore off Craig's snow-encrusted clothes, while Meg brought blankets, then put on water for hot chocolate.

As his brothers wrapped him in the warm blankets, Craig's eyelashes fluttered and he moaned softly.

"Nooo—! Nooo! Don't wanna get up! Bed's so warm…eyes…!"

Meg was just coming in with steaming cups of hot chocolate when she heard Craig. Tears of joy burst forth and streamed down her cheeks, glistening in the firelight. Seeing this, Karl and Mark also lost control, but there were occasions when even boys could cry. Mark was not ashamed—Craig was alive.

Mark got down on his knees, tears flowing freely, and pulled their beloved dog tightly to his breast.

"Thanks, Tito!" was all he could choke out.

Karl, wiping away his tears, looked down at Craig, who was now smiling feebly.

"You lucky little dip," he said affectionately.

. . . . .

It was like nothing in anyone's memory. Even the oldtimers could not remember a snowstorm like this one. It snowed heavily for four days and nights, the winds never letting up. The old house creaked and groaned throughout. When it was all over, three feet of snow smothered the frigid town, and on the fifth day the sun came up in a clear blue sky.

The housebound boys ran from window to window. Their once-familiar yard had been magically transformed into a wondrous snowscape. It looked like the North Pole, and it turned out to be every bit as cold! Now that their near-tragedy was behind them, nothing but fun lay ahead. The snow wasn't melting! Schools would be closed for ages!

"What'll we do first?" Craig burst out. "Have a snowball fight? Make a fort? Build a snowman?"

"Dig a tunnel? It's deep enough! Or go sledding," was Mark's contribution. The possibilities were endless.

They were halfway out the door when their mother spotted them and called out, "Just a minute, you two! Bundle up! It's freezing out there."

Vicky had kept a watchful eye on Craig since his close call. He had a bit of frostbite on one ear, and she was still hesitant to let him go outside.

The brothers paused in their pursuit of happiness, grumbling as they rummaged in the closet for their knee-high boots, mittens, and caps with fold-down earflaps. But at the same time their mother's admonition filled them with delight, because it meant that she was finally giving them their freedom.

The snow was so deep that to go anywhere meant digging a trail several feet down. It was easier, the boys learned, to tunnel under the snow, and in the following days they spent much of their time creating a network of tunnels around the yard. They found time to build several huge snowmen, and later, when the passing cars had packed down the snow on Water Street, they rode their sleds down the hill time and again.

If childhood days are carefree, these were the most carefree of all. No outside chores to do. No schoolwork. No deadlines. Nowhere they had to go. Perhaps never again would Mark and Craig experience such utter joy.

5

Remnants of the huge snowbanks and ruined snow forts were still to be seen as late as August of 1949. In fact, the last traces of the hard-packed snow had just melted when the new school year began.

On the first Saturday after school started, the Mosier brothers had stayed home to enjoy their freedom. Usually they would join their mother on her morning errands, but Alice, the ironing lady, was here today. It was always fun to watch her work and listen to her trill, little-girl voice.

Just now Mark was fixing himself a snack while Alice trilled on animatedly. Tito was under foot as always. At the moment he was hoping for a dropped morsel, as Mark was spreading his bread generously with peanut butter.

The rumble came first, out of the distance. Both boys stopped what they were doing, looking at each other in silent wonder. The house made a sudden lurch, and Mark's bread fell off the counter, narrowly missing Tito. Dishes crashed to the floor. The dog took off like a shot, oblivious of the treat that lay within his grasp. The kitchen door had popped open and Tito was gone, not to be seen or heard from in several days.

In a panic, Alice herded the boys out the door and onto the back porch.

A deafening roar descended upon them. The steps rose and fell, the garage appeared to be leaning toward them, and the ground was moving like a roller coaster.

Alice was making strange, unintelligible chirping sounds. She seemed unable to speak in words the boys could understand. But with her stubby fingers she prodded them down the undulating steps and out into the middle of the driveway. Overhead, power lines were popping and snapping like bullwhips.

Next to the driveway the neighbor's chimney was collapsing. Bricks were landing all around them. Alice held the boys tightly to her breast and bent protectively over them. All of a sudden, the pressure of her arms relaxed, and the startled boys watched as she slid to the ground unconscious. A brick had caught her on the back of the head.

Vicky had just left her mother's house on the East Side and was driving down State Street. The traffic lights were in her favor, and soon she was heading south on Capitol Way.

She neither heard nor felt anything at first. But dreamlike, as if in slow motion, the cars ahead began to rise and fall like ships at sea. "What on earth!" she stammered.

Her eyes darted frantically to left and right as she tried to figure out what was happening. With disbelief, she watched as huge concrete sections of the nearest capitol building crashed onto the sidewalk below.

Looming beyond was the capitol dome, topped by its quaint cupola. Olympia's unrivalled landmark, the Legislative Building is almost an exact replica of the one in the nation's capital. As Vicky looked on, the massive building seemed to tilt at an impossible angle, then right itself. Except for the cupola! Its collapse looked imminent, but as the groundswell abated, it must have settled into place, for it remained in its precarious position. Its angle later became a source of bureaucratic ridicule.

Vicky, who had pulled the car over to the curb, sat in stunned silence as she surveyed the chaos all around her. A gigantic crack had opened in the road just in front of where she had stopped. One car had fallen partway into the rift, and its occupants were desperately trying to clamber out. Other people left their cars where they were and ran in all directions, shouting and confused.

"What happened?" someone yelled.

"Earthquake!" came the shouted reply.

Vicky did not think of herself. *The boys!* she thought. *I've got to get home—right now!*

The road was jammed with cars, and in any case she couldn't drive over that crack. She noticed that the broad sidewalk was mostly clear, and she could see that if she wanted to get home in a hurry, that would be her only path. She turned her wheels sharply to the right, hit the gas pedal, and jumped the curb. Only half a block lay between her and the right turn onto Fourteenth Street. It looked like she could make it all the way on the sidewalk, with some weaving to avoid branches and other fallen debris. More than once she had to brake suddenly to avoid hitting the panic-stricken people.

Fourteenth also appeared to be clear. "Thank God!" she breathed, as the car dropped off the curb onto the roadway. To her right she observed a cement monolith from the Insurance Building's roof embedded several feet into the ground. Then it was a left turn onto Water Street.

Vicky's heartbeat quickened as she saw the extent of damage to some of the houses on her street. At Eighteenth Street, she could see that her next-door neighbor's chimney was a pile of rubble.

The scene that met her eyes as she turned into the driveway filled her with alarm. There were Mark and Craig sitting on the ground, cradling a third figure. She jerked to a stop and jumped from the car, which made a protesting lurch forward as her foot left the clutch.

"Mark! Craig! Are you hurt?" Vicky yelled as she ran to them.

"No, Mama—but Alice is! A brick hit her on the head and knocked her out!" Mark said authoritatively.

"She saved us, Mama," Craig added softly as Vicky bent to examine her. "She won't die, will she?"

Vicky had had some first aid training during the war. She checked the unconscious woman's pulse. "No, honey. It's just a bad bump. But what happened to her feet?" The soles of both Alice's feet were cut and bleeding.

"She was ironin' barefoot—must have cut 'em on the broken glass," Mark deduced.

"The poor dear!" Vicky sent Craig for cloth and tape to use as temporary bandages and instructed Mark to pick up the phone and call for an ambulance. The boys instantly obeyed, relieved that Mama had arrived to take charge.

Of course, all the telephone lines were down, so Vicky had to do the best she could without professional medical help. Ambulances were needed everywhere, but few calls got through. As for Alice, she regained consciousness within a few minutes but stayed with the Mosiers as a houseguest for a week. Mark and Craig catered to her every need.

. . . . .

Damages far exceeded early reports. In places the ground had been displaced six feet or more. Fissures had opened, some miles in length; roads everywhere needed extensive filling and resurfacing. Buildings had been leveled, their debris forever scarring pavement and sidewalks. Earthquake drills became a standard part of schoolyard safety education.

But schools opened as usual that Monday.

Long after things had settled down once more, one thing remained to remind the brothers of the fearful event: that teetering cupola, perilously threatening to fall.

PART IV

Night had long since fallen over Kalihiwai Ridge. The moon was high in a cloudless sky, and the sounds of crickets and bufo toads drifted on the cool sea breezes. Unaware of passing time, the Mosier brothers were lost in the past, digging ever deeper into their family memories.

"Well, what have we here?" Craig remarked, taking a tattered envelope from the depths of the cardboard box. Squinting to read the return address, he looked up suddenly at Mark, his glasses slipping down on his nose.

"It's the letter from Ab!" Craig said.

"The one Dad read on Goodman Creek?" Mark was incredulous. "Are you sure?"

"That's the only one *I* know of! It's dated 1952—and look at all the postmarks!" Craig was obviously carried back to another time and place. "Ahhh...the summers in Forks with Grandma and Granddad! Weren't those the greatest times ever?"

"Usually. *That* summer was a little different, though," Mark recalled.

1

The first Saturday of summer vacation arrived, but Mark and Craig were not celebrating. They dragged themselves out of bed reluctantly and met as usual for breakfast. A light drizzle was falling, giving the boys a slight hope that maybe their dad would call off the planned tree cutting. With Karl away at a summer job, this backbreaking chore had fallen squarely on their young shoulders.

No such luck—there was to be no reprieve. There was Ray Mosier already in the kitchen, waiting for them.

"Haven't you lazy little shits eaten yet? Get your butts in gear!" No "Good morning" greeting from good ol' Dad.

As the boys helped themselves to cereal, Ray's barrage escalated with the shrillness of his voice.

"You kids're worthless! I'm gonna teach you what work really is. When I get done, you won't be able to lift your sorry asses into bed! Now *eat!*" He punctuated this last remark with a furious fist to the table, spilling the boys' milk. "*Clean that up!*" he screamed, storming out the kitchen door.

Mark had noticed that his father's right temple was pulsating and reddening, a sure sign that he was suffering from one of his notorious headaches.

The brothers were so accustomed to their father ranting like this that they almost casually cleaned up after him and continued eating. At this moment, their mother came into the kitchen.

"Good morning, boys," she said cheerfully. "Listen. I didn't get a chance to tell you last night, but your grandparents are coming down today."

"Wow! Let's hurry, Mark, so we can finish before they get here!"

"Not only that—they're taking you back to Forks with them on Monday!" Vicky added. Mark and Craig exchanged sudden looks of delight.

The news was the impetus they needed. Their chore now seemed merely a means toward an end, something for which there would be a reward.

New joy touched the boys' lives whenever their grandparents came to visit. And getting to go back with them for several weeks had become the high point of their summers. They would go into the "tall uncut," as Granddad fondly called it. Their grandparents lived in the middle of the wilds of the Olympic Peninsula.

Now they had a mission: to select a tree, fell it, saw it into pieces, split it, and carry as much of it up the hill as possible before their grandparents arrived.

. . . . .

"TIMBERRR!" Ray cried. Birds and small animals scattered at the cracking sound as another tall alder succumbed to the Mosier ax. This part of the task was fun, and since it was where Ray proved his mettle, he did most of the chopping. The boys savored the entire event: the long moment of hesitation following the last stroke of the ax; the resounding snaps as the trunk began to splinter; the final shudder of resistance to its fate; the slow, majestic descent, picking up speed just before contact; and then, the reverberating crash onto the forest floor.

Now the hard work began. Mark and Craig knew the routine well. Ray would assume his supervisory stance, sitting on the fresh alder stump, shouting commands at them.

The boys would each take an ax and start at opposite ends of the downed tree, expertly shearing the limbs cleanly along the trunk. These they would then saw or chop into kindling and stack for carrying up the hill later.

The heaviest work was to section off the main trunk and lift the sections onto the sawhorse for sawing into fireplace logs. They needed their father's help for this, but today he wasn't offering.

"It's high time you pulled your own weight, Craig! You and Mark lift it up!" he fumed.

This was too big a load for little Craig, even though he realized the consequences of failure. Almost at once, he lost his footing and dropped his end of the log, which broke one leg of the sawhorse as it fell. Ray lunged at Craig and knocked him sprawling across the slippery leaves and into a stump.

"You useless little bastard! You'll never amount to anything!

"I oughta—!" Ray was raising a branch threateningly over Craig's cowering, prostrate form.

Behind his back, unseen, Mark picked up his ax and slowly moved toward his father, not knowing for sure what he was going to do. He gritted his teeth. *If he hits Craig—!*

Mark watched as Ray lost his grip on the branch. Raising both hands to his throbbing head, he groaned and sank to his knees in agony.

With considerable relief, Mark dropped the ax and ran to his little brother's side. Craig, who had been knocked around a lot, was quite resilient, and seemed to be little the worse for wear.

The pain consumed Ray and rendered him temporarily harmless to his sons. The as yet undiscovered needle of shrapnel above his temple, working itself ever deeper, was making it more and more difficult for him to function normally.

When he could, he struggled to his feet and blearily wandered off through the woods in the general direction of home, without a backward glance, leaving the boys to their task.

2

Craig was the first one to hear the familiar growl of the engine entering their driveway. He could also hear the crunch of cinder beneath the tires as the car came to a halt in its traditional resting place under the carport attached to the side of the house. "They're here!" he announced to the family.

Tito made it to the car first and was greeting his own favorite visitor, Topsy, the lovable female cocker who accompanied the old folks on each journey to Olympia. Craig was next, followed closely by Mark, with the rest of the family on his heels. Both boys had received a big hug from Grandma when their father arrived on the scene, and the famous "Indian dance" began.

This ritual captivated the boys. It was the closest that Ray and his father ever came to displaying physical affection. They would join hands, jumping up and down and hooting while careening about and turning in circles. Sometimes this would last a minute or more. Excited by this activity, the two dogs would do a dance of their own. All who witnessed this spectacle were vastly entertained. To Mark and Craig, it came to represent an expression of the deep love between the two men; they found it all the more unique because of their own father's apparent lack of affection for them.

Ray's love was thus selective: while his devotion to his father approached adoration, his relationship with his own children seemed to be based on the precept that they had to earn his affection.

. . . . .

Clarence Iowa Mosier was in fine shape for his age, which the boys thought must be considerable. He had ruggedly handsome features accentuated by high cheekbones and a square jaw. His solid frame and erect posture made him seem much taller than his medium height. His rugged good looks were improved by a shock of thick, snow-white hair. Since he had taken an early dislike to his given name, he was known to friends and relatives simply as C.I. The unfortunate moniker had been bestowed upon him when yet a babe in arms, his parents traveling by train through the Midwest in the

1880s. They had passed through Clarence, a pretty little town in Iowa, and as he was a pretty little thing and still unnamed, it seemed to suggest itself most naturally.

C.I. was born in Ohio and raised in Tennessee, where he acquired his accent. The family was large and very poor—he was ten years old before he saw his first dime. He only completed six years of school, but he read voraciously and could recite poems and Negro spirituals from memory. Langdon Smith's epic poem, *Evolution,* was one of his favorites, and he would often repeat it in its entirety on request. At age eighteen, when many of his contemporaries were joining up for the Spanish-American War, he hopped a freight and rode the rods to the West, where he got his start as a lumberjack.

C.I. had taken Hattie Mae Buling as his bride in 1909, and the two of them had formed a lifelong bond that made it impossible for anyone to imagine them not being together. She was ten years his junior and considered herself plain and therefore downright lucky to have made such a fine catch. She worked hard to please him and was selfless and uncomplaining. And she loved to spoil her grandchildren!

"Whatja bring, Grandma?" Craig prodded her.

"Oh, let's see…open the trunk, C.I.!" She guided him to the rear with the boys in hot pursuit.

She reached into a bag and produced candy for Mark and Craig.

"Mom, you know that's not good for them, with their teeth!" came the predictable response from Ray. "Dentist bills will put us in the poorhouse yet!"

Hattie was one person Ray couldn't intimidate. She tossed this off with a shrug, and the boys were gone with the goodies.

The brothers had retreated to the kitchen and were polishing off the last of their grandmother's candy, idly passing the time of day.

"Y'know what I saw the other day?" Craig asked his brother.

"What?"

"I saw another hobo come to the back door!"

"Huh? Are you sure? Craig, you gotta tell me these things!"

"Well, I didn't think it was such a big deal. He went away."

"You mean Mom didn't let him in?" Mark asked.

"No. She just opened the door a crack, and then closed it."

"Thank goodness she's not letting them in!" Mark breathed. "Did you see where he went?"

"Yeah. He took off toward The Playhouse," Craig remembered.

"The Playhouse!" Mark's voice was rising. "Did he go in The Playhouse?"

"Cool it, Mark! He just went back down in the woods."

Mark was contemplating his brother's report. Finally he asked, "You mean you saw him come up to the house from the woods?"

"Yeah. But before he came up to the house, he walked all the way around The Playhouse, real slow, like he was looking for something."

Mark spoke in subdued tones, as if to himself. "We're gonna have to figure out how to stop these bums from bothering Mom."

The boys were silent for some time as they mulled this over. Thoughtfully, Mark phrased his question.

"Craig, you haven't told anyone what we did, have you?"

"'Course not! Why? How about you?"

"Not me. But have you wanted to?" Mark persisted.

"Yeah, sometimes maybe. But there's nobody to tell."

"I was thinking…how about Granddad?"

Granddad was the one person in the world they could tell anything. They enjoyed a mutual trust with him that dated from their earliest memories. Confiding in him was second nature to them, for he never judged the boys harshly and always had the perfect advice. And—most important this time— he had never betrayed a confidence.

"Boy, I'd really like to, but…." Craig trailed off.

"Yeah, I know. It wouldn't be fair to him. My gosh, he'd have to tell someone about a body buried down in our woods!" Mark realized.

"How about just telling him part of it—like the part about the hobo getting Mom?"

"Don't forget, Dad doesn't know anything about Mom feeding the hoboes. Granddad would have to tell his own son!"

Craig absorbed this. "And we promised Mom. It's all over if Dad finds out!"

Both boys really believed their father would kill them if he ever discovered their awful secret.

"So I guess we better not tell him," Mark decided.

"Yeah," Craig agreed.

Saturday night was bridge night whenever "the folks" came. The boys always used these times to obtain family news updates. By eavesdropping on the card-table conversation, they often became privy to valuable information not normally available to them. They would remain in the background, out of sight but never out of earshot.

This particular night was not looking very promising. They had to sit through another retelling (how many times was it?) of the "Ab-Normal" War Story. It was C.I.'s favorite, and Ray never missed an opportunity to tell it again. The story had grown with each recounting, until it was now of epic length and legendary proportions. To hear Ray tell it, you'd think John Normal had saved half the Atlantic fleet, and himself the other half. Of course, Ray *had* won the Congressional Medal of Honor—and Ab had at least been recommended for it—so his proud father drank in every word of the embellished account.

When Ray finally finished, Vicky asked, "Honey, did you ever find out what happened to John?"

"Nope. Last time I saw him was at the Red Star Club in Murmansk. Haven't heard a thing about him since. Don't know whether he's dead or alive...."

The evening wore on. Ray, his father, and Vicky were well into the bourbon supply. They were getting disapproving looks from tee-totaling Hattie, who peered at them over the rims of her glasses. She was not a nag, but fancied that she had higher standards than the others, and was not above moralizing. She still joined in the conversation, although she found it increasingly tedious. Ray naturally blamed his mother's lack of interest on her sobriety.

"Ray, tell me about your work. How's it going at the capitol?" Hattie queried.

"Great, Mom. In fact, I'm glad you asked. There's been an interesting development I've been wanting to tell you folks."

The boys' ears pricked up. An interesting development! It seemed all they ever heard from Ray about his state job was complaints. Vicky, who had to bear the brunt of his evening harangues, smiled knowingly. "He's going to be lieutenant governor!" she gushed.

"Honey!" Ray silenced her. "For Pete's sake! Let me tell it!"

But it was too late. There was nothing for Ray to do but continue limply.

"Dad, you probably heard that Jacobson had a heart attack. Well, his doctors are making him resign, and they're talking about me for the appointment. In fact, I think I'm number one in line. And if I get it, several of the higher-ups have already suggested me to run for governor in two years," he slurred.

"When will you know?" asked Hattie excitedly.

"They figure it'll be announced in time for Monday's *Daily Olympian*."

"If that don't beat all!" C.I. hollered. He jumped spryly to his feet, pulling Ray up, and the boys were treated to a second Indian dance on the same day!

"This calls for a celebration!" Hattie said, caught up in the fervor of the moment.

"Let's plan a big day down the bay tomorrow!" Vicky suggested. "We can get corn on the cob from Mobb's."

"I'll pick up some big crabs from the dock," Ray contributed.

"Oh, yes! A big crab feed! I'll bake a couple blackberry pies," Hattie added.

"Lemme see. What's left?" C.I. mused.

"How 'bout the whisky!" was Ray's instant response.

"How 'bout Old Grandad?" said C.I. with feeling.

"Nothin' but the best, huh?"

In the next room, Mark and Craig were contemplating doing a dance of their own. The conversation filled them with sudden animation. They loved going down the bay, and here they were going on the last day before leaving for Forks! And if all this wasn't enough to take in, someday they might even live in the governor's mansion!

3

Forks! The old familiar butterflies fluttered in their stomachs for the first time since last summer. They were anticipating the long three-hour drive, every part of which they knew by heart and loved. They could name every little town, each river they crossed on the way. And every trip brought new and intriguing tales about these places from their grandparents.

The Mosier brothers were already in the car, waiting impatiently to get started. Ray was gone to work and had already said his goodbyes. Vicky was thinking of the boys and trying to get the old folks moving.

"We'll telephone you tonight if there's any news about Ray," she called as Hattie backed out of the carport.

Mark thought, *Wow, no Dad for three weeks! No chores, no screaming, nothing to do but have fun!*

At the same time, Craig was thinking, *Geeminy! No beatings from Dad. I'll really miss Mom, though.*

"Why so quiet, boys? Cat got your tongue?" C.I. asked.

"Where we gonna stop for lunch, Granddad?" Since Mark did not want to admit his true thoughts, this seemed like a good response. Especially since Mark was always thinking about food.

"Probably in Montesano. That little place—you know, C.I.—where we ate on the way down," Hattie offered.

"We et the food we ne'er had et, and 'round and 'round we flew," C.I. misquoted, to the delight of his young listeners. This was his usual prelude to a great feast, and was the best recommendation they knew.

. . . . .

They came to the "Y," as they called the intersection where the road branched off to the Olympic Highway from the more familiar route down the bay. Whenever they took the highway on the left, it was a moment of elation, for this was the ultimate path to adventure in their young lives.

"Throughout

"This world

"Of toil

"And sin

"Your head

"Grows bald

"But not

"Your chin.

"Burma Shave."

Mark read aloud as the familiar red and white signposts flashed by. The same message had been there for years, and both boys knew it meant lunch was not far ahead.

"Looky there, boys! That there's another one o' them stump farms!" C.I. gestured off to the right as they passed a fenced-in field dotted with numerous tree stumps about waist high. They took it in. There were no crops planted, only grass, and it didn't look suitable for grazing cattle. Since the boys knew their grandfather had infinite knowledge, they accepted without question that, apparently, some farmers cultivated stumps!

McCleary. Elma. Satsop. They passed through each small town, taking them farther from home and nearer their storied destination.

After the lunch stop in Montesano, it was on to Aberdeen and Hoquiam, adjoining ports on Grays Harbor—gray water and gray buildings.

Past Hoquiam the road took a sharp curve to the north and headed into the untamed wilderness of the Olympic Peninsula. The next outpost of civilization would be Humptulips, which marked the halfway point of their trip.

"Here we go, into the tall uncut!" was C.I.'s predictable observation as the towering fir trees seemed to close in overhead, the sky becoming a narrow slit above. This long, isolated stretch of highway might seem monotonous to many, but not to the Mosier brothers, exposed as they had been to their grandfather's colorful imagination. As the miles rolled by, they dreamed of the adventures to be had in those marvelous depths of forest, and it prepared them for what lay ahead.

Quinault was a small Indian village carved out of the forest on the edge of a large lake of the same name. Here the highway made another bend, to the west toward the great Pacific Ocean. Next came Queets.

"You boys ever hear how this place got its name?" They had, many times, but he loved to tell it, and they always liked to hear it.

"No, Granddad!" Craig fibbed.

"Well, they was these two fellers a-fishin' down there in the river. One was a Swede and t'other was a Scandihoovian. They wasn't havin' much luck, and it was gettin' late in the day. So the Swede feller says to the other feller, 'Let's call eet queets!' And by golly, it's been Queets to this day!"

Past Queets they would get their first tantalizing glimpses of the ocean, quick views of the roiling waves through gullies worn into the rugged coastline. Numerous streams rose in the Olympic Mountains to the east and carved their pathways to the sea, testimony to the heavy rainfall in the region. Speeding by in the car, Mark and Craig would crane their necks to see whatever they could.

The last chance to stop at the ocean was at Ruby Beach. Grandma would usually give in to the boys' pleadings and pull off at the little store by the wayside. Promising not to be long, they would run down the trail to the gravelly shore and drink in the spectacle: Abbey Rock rising vertically just offshore, capped in green, with a few straggly firs; Destruction Island, almost invisible far out on the horizon, its lighthouse winking at them through the mist; the long, foamy foreshore stretching out to the combers breaking in the distance.

"Maybe we can come camping down here this time," Mark suggested.

"Yeah, neat!" Craig said as they ran back up the beach.

After Ruby Beach, they were on the home stretch. The road went inland again and followed the Hoh River for a few miles. At the bridge over the Hoh they could see Hell Roaring Creek living up to its name, tumbling tumultuously into the big stream. When they passed the road leading deep into the Olympic Mountains to Jackson Ranger Station, they knew they were almost there.

On the edge of their seats, they leaned as the car rounded the final bend. As they entered the mill camp, they were deluged by sensory delights. The sights, smells, and sounds were all-pervasive. First they saw the clouds of steam rising from their Granddad's shingle mill. The pungent aroma of cedar invaded their nostrils. The rhythmic scream of the saws assaulted their ears as they drew closer.

The little settlement was a model of self-sufficiency. The mill provided employment and power to all residents. A large water tower supplied all the water they could use. Ramshackle housing was available to some workers and their families. In marked contrast to these shacks, the owners had built themselves fine, though rustic, homes. The forest had been pushed back far enough to accommodate perhaps a dozen structures along this isolated quarter-mile of highway. Granddad would say that if a passing motorist blinked, he'd miss this wide spot in the road. But to Mark and Craig it was a universe unto itself.

"Here we are, back in our ol' stompin' grounds!" came C.I.'s gravelly announcement, as Hattie pulled into their driveway.

4

Memories of early childhood flooded back every summer when the boys arrived at the camp. After all, their love of the place was rooted in the long-ago time, dimly remembered, when they had lived there during the war—memories such as the time Mark had walked into an open cesspool and had sunk from sight, barely rescued in time by his uncle; memories of the "indoor outhouse" whose hole—but not smell—was covered by a real toilet seat in the tumbledown shack they had lived in; warm, fuzzy memories of trips to beaches, mountains, and rivers, feeding wild elk from their hands, the first tentative penetrations of the trackless wilderness around the camp.

The car pulled into the garage and the boys jumped out. The back porch had been hewn from an enormous stump, into which steps had been cut. Hattie was opening the back door as the boys manhandled the bags up onto the stump. As the door swung open, they all heard the ringing.

"Oh, fiddle!" Hattie complained. "It's the telephone." She bustled to answer it.

"Damn thing. Never did see the need for 'em. Made for women to gab on!" C.I. grumbled.

"Hello?" Hattie always yelled into the telephone in those days of bad connections.

"Mom? I've got big news. Is Dad there?" It was Ray, and he was barely audible.

"Is that you, Ray? I can't hardly hear you! Can you speak up?" Then, to C.I.: "I think it's Ray! Come quick!" She held the receiver so that he could hear, too.

"I got the job! Lieutenant governor! Listen to this headline in the paper: 'MOSIER LANDS NO. 2 SPOT'!"

Over the crackling interference, they got the message.

"Well I'll be!" C.I. cried, jumping up and down. "That's worth thirty years o' hard livin'!"

"What's that, Dad? Oh, yeah!" Ray laughed as he recognized another of his father's offbeat witticisms. "I'll send you this article so you can read it—it's a long one, and it makes me sound pretty good."

C.I. wrestled the phone away from Hattie, an idea coming to him.

"How long before you start?"

"A week from today, Dad," Ray responded.

"Say, son! S'pose we might take that fishin' trip up the coast we been talkin' about come Sattiday? Might be a long time comin', otherwise!"

"Gee, Dad—that would be great! Let's see—I could drive up Friday night—as long as I get back by Sunday night. I'll see if I can work it out!"

Long-distance phone calls being expensive, they were always short and to the point, and this was no exception. After they hung up, C.I. felt moved to modify his earlier sentiment.

"Shore glad I talked you into gettin' us one o' them gadgets, Hattie Mae!"

. . . . .

C.I. was foreman on the swing shift, starting at 3:00 P.M. The house was just a stone's throw from the mill. After the phone call, he had just enough time to get into his work clothes and walk down.

"Time to mosey on down and see if I can cause any mischief," he announced. "You boys want to tag along?"

Mark and Craig didn't need to be asked. They never missed accompanying him on his mill rounds, and this was their first visit in a whole year.

"Sure, Granddad!" they chimed.

The two brothers ran ahead. On their first visit each year, it was their custom to take a quick tour of the mill and catch up with their grandfather later. Their faces were familiar to nearly all the millworkers, many of whom were relatives, and they would be hailed and warmly greeted as they passed from one section to another. They literally enjoyed the "run of the mill," but they never really thought much about it. Possibly it was because they were the part-owner's grandchildren, but whatever the reason, they were never chastised or berated for placing themselves in such potential danger.

As they walked down the road, they could see one of the big logging trucks about to dump its load of logs into the mill pond on one side of the mill. The donkey engine was huffing and puffing, angling the truck bed until the logs broke loose and rolled thunderously down the ramp and made a stupendous splash that often doused the boys. This time the water sprayed the other way, wetting down the side of the mill facing them across the pond and soaking Mike the pond man. Mike spent his days walking the floating logs, maneuvering them with his long, spiked pole toward the bullchain that lifted them one by one to the giant saw above. As the boys watched, Mike shook his fist angrily at the donkey engine operator.

"Sacre bleu! May you roast in hell!" came faintly to their ears, even above the din surrounding them. Mike was a French Canadian, rather rare in these parts, and was often the subject of ridicule, just because he was different. But Mark and Craig didn't make fun of him, and they were his only friends. At that moment, Mike recognized them, and his angry gesture melted into a wave as he gave them a broad grin.

Mike deftly hopped from log to log with his hobnail boots. He set about positioning a huge cedar at the base of the bullchain. The hungry hook gripped the log, and it began its ascent up the V-shaped trough.

"Wow! Look at the size of that log!" Mark exclaimed. "That must be the biggest one yet!"

Craig was already in a dead run. "C'mon, let's watch 'em cut it up!" he yelled back over his shoulder.

They ran around the pond and up the long ramp on the highway side of the mill. At the top was a little door. As they entered, they could see the massive log just approaching the top of the bullchain opposite them. The bullsaw, biggest of all the saws, was set at right angles to the logs and would cut them into sections that would then be quartered by a much smaller saw close to where the boys were now standing.

Both of these operations were manually controlled. In the case of the bullsaw, the operator stood directly opposite the saw, with the log passing between him and the saw. When the log was positioned correctly, he would pull on an overhead handle, and the saw would move toward him and begin cutting the log. Cutting complete, he would push back on the handle, and the saw would retreat again into its alcove.

Each time the brothers watched this—the most spine-tingling event of all the mill's operations—they were reminded of what had happened to their cousin Jed when he was a bullsawyer. The great saw had broken loose from its fittings as it was approaching a log. In the flash of an eye, the spinning blade cut a swath right through the side of the mill and into the pond below, taking Jed's entire right arm with it. Jed had been fitted with an artificial arm, a metal contraption that worked with a series of straps stretched over his shoulder and back. For a hand, he had a stainless steel hook that he could open and close by a particular combination of muscle movements. Since he had learned to use this hook with great dexterity, he still worked at the mill, stoking the boilers with the cast-off wood and sawdust.

After quartering, the sections were carried by a smaller bullchain up another level to the shingle saws. This was a single row of six or eight manned stations, each with a shingle saw mounted on the left. As a block came up the bullchain, the sawyer would place it in position to saw the shingles. Two trimming saws protruded about an inch above the working surface directly in front of him. As his shingle saw went to work cutting shingles from the block, the sawyer would reach to his left without looking, take the newly cut shingle, trim its rough edges on the saws before him, and drop it in the chute to the packers below.

Not infrequently, the packers would receive something else along with the shingles: a severed finger or thumb! These could be hacked off without warning if sawyers got careless for any reason; their risk increased geometrically when sawyers came to work following one of their infamous drinking binges.

Mark and Craig knew that the loss of three fingers meant the loss of this "frontline" job. But since no one ever got fired at the mill (so far as they knew), this meant being relegated to the lower-level job of shingle packer. The boys were never certain whether the change in position was merely punitive or had to do with the actual ability to peel those shingles off the saw. They knew from observation, however, that few of their uncles and cousins were in possession of all their original digits. They would watch this operation with fascination until the high-pitched whining of the saws made their ears ring. Then they would run down the sawdust-encrusted stairs to the packing shed.

As they rounded the staircase into the shed, they were happy to see that their Uncle Wes was on the job. It had been several years since Wes had lost his third finger, and he had become the best packer of them all. They could tell by his bleary-eyed stare that he wasn't in great shape, but that didn't slow him down.

"Well, well! How are you boys? It's been a long time. I hear we're goin' up the coast in my boat this weekend, eh?" He could carry on a conversation without missing a beat. His hands were a blur as the boys watched him fit the shingles into perfect place as if assembling a jigsaw puzzle at lightning speed. He expertly banded the completed pack and heaved it onto the conveyor that would take it to the kiln.

The three chatted amiably for a few minutes while Wes took a smoke break. "Oh, yeah! We can't wait," Mark answered. "Did you hear about our Dad?"

"Sure did—that's big news around here! Can't wait to hobnob with the Number Two man!" Wes and Ray had been close in their youth, and a bond still existed between them. At one time, Wes had been the hope of the entire Buling clan, graduating Phi Beta Kappa from college and rising in business, before alcohol took its toll and reduced him to his present lowly state, working in the family shingle mill, living in a rundown barracks-type shack, headquarters of the camp binges.

Next on their tour was the kiln. Massive sliding doors rolled open easily on greased ball bearings, allowing entry and egress of thirty-foot wide carts loaded ten feet high with the freshly packed shingles. The carts were mounted on wheels and were pushed by hand along railroad-type tracks that led through the kiln into the shingle shed beyond, where they awaited shipment. The same power that ran the mill generated steam to heat this kiln and "cure" the shingles, the final step in the process.

The boys never missed a pass through the kiln's sixty-foot length. As they slid the door closed behind them, the heat and humidity enveloped them like a long-forgotten womb. Darkness dictated caution as they made their way through the narrow space between the wall and the ragged edge of the stacked shingles. Groping for the door on the far end, they would slide it open just far enough to get out. Covered with a layer of warm moisture, they would be shocked by the blast of cooler outside air.

Before them now lay the cavernous shingle shed, where the stacks of shingles reached for the rafters, awaiting the arrival of the truck that would carry them to the railhead. Before their summer visit was over, Mark and Craig would spend hours climbing high on top of these cedar monuments.

But this was not the case today. Already wet and not wanting to cool off just yet, the brothers were drawn by the sound of the steam pipes. This was where excess steam was occasionally vented in rhythmic blasts from the mill into the open air. The pipes extended beneath the pilings at the end of the shingle shed, and were the perfect height for young boys to enjoy the clouds of steam they produced. Even on the warmest summer days, billowing steam would create an environment not unlike a battleground. The immediate area around the pipes was desolate. The ground was barren of any growth, and in years past the boys had fought many an imaginary battle with unseen enemies.

The steam, looking so invitingly clean, always left an oily residue all over them, so they would have to clean up afterward. It also meant taking a lighthearted scolding from their grandmother, a small price to pay for this much fun—and a trifle compared to their Dad's rages.

5

Wilderness encroached on the camp along both sides of the highway. Nearly impenetrable forest began at the back door of each dwelling. One of the top priorities for Mark and Craig was to renew their acquaintance with the woods immediately behind their grandparent's house.

The next day found them walking The Stack, a mammoth, jumbled pile of ancient gray logs on the edge of the jungle at the rear of the Mosier home. They were with Gary Gent, a friend who lived in a little cabin at the far end of the camp. Gary had just regaled them with the story of how his father had shot a good-sized elk from his own back porch. Such tales brought home to the citified brothers just how wild the country around here really was.

If they could only keep Gary from dallying, they had their minds set on making a deep thrust into the tall uncut, maybe even as far as the Bogachiel River. Gary seemed bent on exploring every nook and cranny along the way, while the brothers had grander exploits to undertake.

"Where is he now?" Craig asked Mark, already exasperated.

"Up a tree, I think. I'll go back and see."

Progress had been excruciatingly slow, mostly thanks to Gary, but also because it was tough going. Not only was the underbrush thick, but fallen trees made it impossible to maintain a steady course.

They were always getting turned around, and many times would come out of the woods to find themselves behind the mill, where a wooden dam backed up the water for the millpond.

As Mark approached the tree he figured Gary had climbed, there came a horrendous roar out of the dense growth nearby. Mark and Craig froze where they stood. They heard the crashing sounds that could only be made by a large, heavy animal. As the thundering roar grew suddenly louder, they knew it was almost upon them.

They were still rooted to the spot when Craig yelled, "Mark, look! A bear cub!"

Mark was at the base of the tree. To his left, at a distance of perhaps fifteen feet, he spotted the cub. The crashing ceased, and Mark turned his head slowly, deliberately, to the right. There, rising on its hind legs, ferocious eyes flashing, deadly fangs bared and dripping, was a giant brown bear, poised to attack.

Mark realized in an instant that they were between the mother bear and her cub—and in real danger. The final, earsplitting roar fell upon them, shaking them to the core of their beings. It was a death knell, the very sound of doom, and to run would be useless.

Suddenly there was a shadowy figure, only half-seen, moving with fierce determination. It scooped up the cub from behind Craig and set out running with it—*toward the mother!*

As the figure leapt past, Mark recognized Mike the pond man. In stupefaction, the boys watched as Mike lunged desperately to deliver the cub to its mother without coming into range of those fearsome claws.

But the bear's attack had already begun, and her forward momentum was irreversible. As Mike dropped the cub at her feet, a savage swipe of her mighty paw raked across his face and neck and sent him sprawling. Mother and cub disappeared again into the brush. Before the brothers could even get to Mike, they heard a cracking and snapping overhead, and Gary came crashing painfully to the ground, groaning and holding his ribcage.

. . . . .

After the bear incident, Mike's standing in the little community was never the same. The ghastly crimson scar down the left side of his face marked him as the true hero he was. There was no more teasing, and he was made a full-fledged member of the camp, honored and respected by all.

Gary, his broken ribs quickly healed, vowed never again to let Mark and Craig drag him along on one of their crazy expeditions.

The Mosier brothers had been delivered from certain death. But the lure of the tall uncut would live on in their hearts.

6

The rest of that week Mark and Craig were content to visit with their aunts, uncles, and cousins, telling and retelling the story of their close call with the monstrous she-bear. In time the tale built to the status of a legend, and heads would turn to watch in awe as Mike passed. His quiet, unassuming manner was not affected by his notoriety, and he settled into a happy routine at the mill.

Friday came all too fast for Mark and Craig, who were anxious to go on the excursion but were having mixed feelings because their father was coming.

They were just finishing off another of their grandmother's great dinners: chicken and dumplings, corn on the cob, and homemade apple pie, when they heard the familiar toot-toot of the family car pulling in. Both boys simultaneously experienced the sinking sensation that always came with the arrival of their father. The unfettered freedom that was theirs only when at the camp was now in jeopardy.

"Hi, Mom, hi, Dad. Boy, something smells good! Am I in time for dinner? Oh, hi, boys—you need to wash the car. It got all muddy on the trip up," was Ray's greeting as he came in through the front door. "Oh, and go get my suitcase out of the trunk!"

"Pull up a chair and I'll dish you up," said Hattie.

"We almost cut your place out of the table!" chuckled C.I. Then, more seriously: "We're gettin' up and at 'em real early, son, so we'd best turn in soon's we can! I got your Uncle Ray to stand the rest of my shift." Ray had been named for his mother's older brother, and since he had grown up close by, he had lived for years with the humiliation of being called "Little Ray." Perhaps now, at last, he would get his due respect.

"Okay, Dad. What time are we getting up?" Ray asked.

"Wes oughta be here at four, if he manages to stay sober. Figger we should get our gear together tonight so we're ready when he moseys in. He wants to be on the water at first light. Hattie made us some fixin's to eat on the way."

"The boys have quite a story to tell you, Ray! I can tell they're chompin' at the bit," Hattie said. It wasn't entirely true, since even a life-threatening encounter might earn their father's unpredictable wrath.

Mark began reluctantly, but the oft-told story now rolled easily off his tongue, and the excitement of its telling was infectious. Even Ray was soon caught up in it. It was beginning to look like, for once, they might get by without even a derogatory comment.

"You boys are going to have to learn to be more careful when you're out in these woods! Why, when I was your age—"

"Now, Ray, never you mind! You didn't have it so bad. And we're just glad the boys are okay. They had a big scare." Hattie had the last word.

By this time, she had piled Ray's plate high and he concentrated on eating. He made short work of the feast, and finished by repeating one of his father's popular witticisms. "I'll be all right if I have an early breakfast!

. . . . .

There was a faint glimmer of light on the eastern horizon as they pulled into the little coastal village of La Push. The Indian settlement occupies the mouth of the Quillayute River, formed by the juncture of the Soleduck, Calawah, and Bogachiel Rivers near Forks, from which that town takes its name.

They arrived on the dock loaded down with gear and stopped at a slip that contained a craft whose seaworthiness was questionable, to say the least. Ray, the former navy man, inspected it dubiously. It looked like an accident about to happen.

"You actually go to sea in this thing, Wes? Even with no cabin?"

"Well, I know it ain't what you're used to, Guvner. But she's shipshape enough for me. And don't worry—I got life jackets for everyone." Wes' feelings were hurt. This boat was his pride and joy, and one his few possessions, since he habitually drank away his paycheck.

Wes busied himself priming the engine while Ray and the boys stowed the gear up under the bow. It was an eighteen-footer that had seen better days. The 10-horsepower outboard didn't look much better, but with Wes' tender coaxing it sputtered into life and was soon idling rhythmically.

Beyond the breakwater protecting the small boat harbor from the open ocean, today the sea was calm and smooth. *Thank goodness,* Ray thought. On most days the Pacific here was a choppy mass of whitecaps scudding across the tops of mountainous, undulating swells.

As the boat slipped down with the current, they emerged from the breakwater. Wes putted offshore about a mile, then steered a course south toward their destination.

"Like I told you fellers before, I know this really fine place to camp right inside the mouth of Goodman Creek," Wes shouted above the noisy outboard.

"How far is it?" Ray hollered.

"Goodman be about eight miles as the crow flies," C.I. advised. "'Course, we cain't fly. If we hug the coast, maybe ten miles."

Wes nodded. C.I. lit up a cigar. Ray passed out the Oly beer; he thought they just might survive ten miles of this, if it only stayed calm.

Mark and Craig were taking in the panorama that was unfolding as the little boat churned slowly down the coast.

It was an incredibly rocky, rugged coastline. Past La Push there was no place a boat could possibly land safely. High cliffs descended vertically to meet the sea, jagged headlands jutting out toward them. All signs of civilization vanished. There were also numerous exposed rocks far out from the coast, which meant navigating these waters was fraught with danger.

But Wes knew every rock from his previous trips and was expertly maneuvering the boat among them. Hopefully, he would remain sober long enough to get them where they were going.

C.I. was well into his second beer. Taking note of the rising swells, he launched into one of his favorite verses:

> The *Piebald Kate* went down that day
> With all that sailed thereon
> And dumped us in an oyster bed,
> Both me and brother John.

"Dad, this is no time—" Ray protested nervously.

> Both rubber boots and rubber coats
> And um-ber-ellas stout
> Couldn't keep the rain from soakin' through—
> Couldn't keep the moisture out!

Ray was beginning to wonder how he'd allowed himself to be talked into this venture. The swells were now so large that they would lose sight of land as they slipped into the trough.

Wes had been keeping them apprised of their progress, however. Occasionally he would shout out the names of familiar landmarks.

"There's the Quillayute Needles!"

"We're passin' Giant's Graveyard!"

"Toleak Point! Not far now!"

At the top of a particularly immense swell, Wes called out, "Thar she be!"

He indicated a point on the coast that looked no more accessible than any other they had seen since leaving La Push. He pulled the little boat hard to the left and headed in. Soon they could make out the towering rocks that dotted the entrance—or what Ray figured must be the entrance—to Goodman Creek. Their massive bulk rose near at hand, waves alternately crashing, then receding, exposing sea kelp and barnacles adhering to their lower surfaces.

"Hold on tight, fellers!" Wes warned his already wary passengers. "We're gonna have to ride the swells in past these rocks! The tide'll help push us in." Wes had timed the trip to coincide with the incoming tide, since the creek could not be entered at any other time. To buck the forceful currents of an outgoing tide would have been foolhardy and treacherous. Using great skill born of experience, Wes deftly rode the waves around and through the maze of obstructions and safely into the narrow, deep channel.

Suddenly all was calm again. Silence descended so abruptly that the thunderous roar still echoed in their ears. There was no crashing surf, no tumultuous rise and fall, as the boat glided up the stream. On both sides, sheer cliffs rose from the water's edge straight up and out of sight. Smooth, dark green water slipped quietly beneath them, testifying to the unknown depth. The occupants of the boat were rendered momentarily speechless by this instant transformation from chaos to serenity.

The putt-putt of the engine was all they heard for awhile, echoing faintly off the canyon walls. Wes was the first to speak.

"By God, that was a sonofabitch! That calls for another beer!"

Ray was aghast, hearing the words from afar. The North Atlantic had been bad enough. "Damn! I thought we were gonna swamp back there—look at all the water we took on! Is it always that rough?"

"Nope, never the times I've been up. Now, how about that beer?"

Ray fumbled for the church key, opened a bottle, and handed it shakily to the man at the helm. Next he opened one for himself, looking at his previous one that had drained its contents into the bottom of the boat, where he must have dropped it during their entry.

Now recovering his senses, Craig piped up, "I don't see any place to camp, Uncle Wes."

"Yeah, do we have to climb up these cliffs to find a spot?" Mark added worriedly. He was craning his neck in a futile effort to see the top.

"Hang onto your britches, lads. You're in for a treat—just around that bend in the river up ahead," Wes assured them.

7

The canyon walls seemed to meet where Wes had gestured, and it looked to the boys' untrained eyes that the stream narrowed even further and might even be impassable. They rounded the bend.

Once again they were jolted as the scene dramatically changed. The stream broadened, and the cliffs fell away behind them, opening up before them into a pristine valley of unbelievable lushness. Thick Spanish moss covered the trees, draped over their branches like green blankets, hanging even into the stream. On their left was meadowland, and on the right was a wide gravel bar, well sheltered by huge forest sentinels. Wes made a flourish toward the inviting spot.

"What did I tell you, lads? Does it meet your fancy?"

Mark and Craig thought that it would be a grand place to make camp.

"Neat-o!" was Craig's reaction. Mark nodded his agreement.

Wes steered the boat ashore in the now shallow stream, neatly beaching it in a tiny cove behind the gravel bar.

"Looks like good fishin' right here off the bar!" C.I. observed.

"Can you picture me fishin' off anythin' else?" Wes joked.

Laughs all around. Poking fun at himself was one of Wes' saving graces.

"I ever tell you the definition of a pun?" C.I. asked. He had, of course—many times. But they all knew he was going to tell them again.

"It's the lowest form of human speech…". C.I.'s way of trailing off made his brand of humor unique, and even though often retold, his little vignettes were always welcome.

With that, they all hopped out of the boat and made ready to set up camp. Without being told, Mark and Craig started off-loading the gear.

"We gonna lay our sleeping bags on the gravel?" Mark said, surveying the large waterworn rocks.

"What's the matter, weren't you expecting to rough it?" Ray taunted.

"I got an idea," Craig said to Mark, ignoring their father's comment.

"Oh, shut up, stupid," Mark grunted as he tried to lift the heavy cooler from inside the boat. "Help me lift this!"

"We can pull off some moss for a mattress!" Craig persisted.

"Mattress? What'd I do, raise a couple of pantywaists? You're camping in the wilds and you need all the comforts of home! Maybe we oughta go back for the sheets!" Ray was merciless, but the boys had learned to accept his insults and go on about their business. They knew they were usually safe from physical harm when others were around.

As soon as the boys were out of earshot of their father, Mark gave Craig a rare compliment.

"Once in a lifetime, Craig, you come up with a halfway decent idea!"

They quickly finished unloading. Their grandfather surreptitiously approached and whispered to them, "Get enough for me, too, boys—my old bones could use a cushion!"

The brothers mounted the bank nearby. The moss was thickest on ancient fallen logs, and they began tearing it off in long sections. As they became more practiced, they could remove patches so large they were almost too heavy to carry. They learned to position themselves one on each end, and shake the section like a rug, knocking loose the clinging dirt and crawling insects adhering to the underside. This greatly reduced the weight, enabling them to carry the pieces relatively intact to the campsite below. Four trips provided a thick, wonderfully soft layer, just large enough for three sleeping bags. Wes and Ray, after all, were "roughing it" and had no need for such luxury.

C.I. was busily preparing his fishing gear, while Ray and Wes got into serious drinking. Wes' cheap bourbon was all they had brought, but after all that excitement it didn't matter. Booze was booze.

A few drinks, and maybe we'll be off the hook, Mark thought.

Mark politely interrupted the conversation. "'Scuse me, Uncle Wes. Can Craig and I unfold your canvas canoe and explore up the stream a ways?"

"Not before you make a fire pit, you can't!" Ray cut in.

"Aw, Ray! We got lotsa time for that. Let the lads have their fun while its still daylight," Wes argued.

Ray's grunt signaled his grudging acquiescence. The longsuffering boys had won again, for the moment. They hurriedly assembled the flimsy craft, each grabbed a paddle, and they headed upstream.

Wes hollered after them. "Whatever you do, lads, don't go *downstream!*"

"Don't worry, Uncle Wes, we know!" Mark shouted back as they approached the first bend.

As the bend of the river cut them off from the sights and sounds behind them, they entered their own private world once again. The light little craft skimmed swiftly and easily over the surface of the stream. Rays of sunlight played in its crystalline depths, producing a kaleidoscope of color as rainbow trout darted in and out among the rocks.

The rippling water ahead announced rapids, and headway became more difficult.

"Paddle harder, Craig!" Mark ordered. But their forward momentum had ceased.

An eddy in the current sent the canoe toward the gravel bank to one side. Mark was at the bow and saw that he would have to get out.

"I'll try to pull it past the rapids. It looks like they end up there—I can see still water."

It was easier than they thought. Soon, the stream bottom dropped from view and a wide, sylvan pool spread out before them. Mark jumped aboard and they floated lazily out on its idyllic surface.

About halfway across the breadth of the pool, Mark spied something.

"My gosh! Is that a house?"

"There's a fence," Craig noticed. "Could someone live this far out in the sticks?"

Of the same mind, the boys paddled rapidly over to have a closer look. As they grew nearer, it was apparent that the place was long abandoned. The split-rail fence had collapsed in many places. They beached the canoe and clambered onto the bank. The cabin, which had looked intact, on closer inspection was found to be in a shambles. The door hung precariously on a single leather hinge, the roof was caving in all around, and the floor was covered by many years' accumulation of leaves and twigs.

"It's an old homestead!" Mark exclaimed.

Craig was first inside. "Hey, what's that on the wall?"

They peered at what seemed to be wallpaper.

"I think it's an old newspaper," Mark observed.

"'Seattle Post...'—I dunno. Can't read it, it's all torn and faded."

"Wait! Here's a date. 'May...'—something—'...1891'!" Mark read in awe.

"Wow! Someone lived here that long ago?"

The brothers looked around inside but found nothing more of value. The newspaper crumbled at their touch, so they gave up any thought of taking a sample back to their elders.

Outside the cabin, Craig mused, "I wonder what they ate."

"Musta lived off the land. There's fish in Goodman Creek. Elk and deer for meat. And maybe they even had a garden."

Craig squinted thoughtfully. "Look over there. Rows of little trees!"

They approached the stunted growth and saw the miniature fruit.

"Crab apples," Mark announced, having seen them before around the camp.

"Let's try one!"

Craig picked one of the biggest apples he could find, still so small he could completely enclose it in his fist.

"Yech! Sour!" Craig complained through puckered lips. But he didn't spit it out, marveling at this insight into the hardship those old pioneers must have endured.

"Let's take some back to show 'em what we found," Mark suggested. "I wonder if Uncle Wes knows this place is here?"

The boys filled their pockets and headed back to the canoe.

8

The whitewater rapids picked up the canoe and shot them downstream. As the campsite hove into view, a rising plume of smoke greeted them, and the enticing smell of pan-fried trout reached their nostrils. The sudden warmth of the place welcomed them as if they were returning home after a long journey.

"Wow, look! Granddad must have made a fire!" Craig said.

"And caught some trout. Yum! Let's go get some," Mark added enthusiastically.

As they slid onto the gravel bar, they could hear the fish sizzling in the pan. C.I. walked over to pull the canoe up, and whispered confidentially to the boys.

"Your Dad and Wes are three sheets to the wind, boys. Figger they won't be interested in fish for awhile. Grab yourself some eatin' irons—the grub's about ready!"

"Thanks for making the fire, Granddad!" said Mark as they followed him back.

"You brats're lettin' your Granddad do all the work!" Ray slurred in their direction. No welcome back, no curiosity about what they might have found, only another reprimand.

"Let 'em be, Ray. The lads have been explorin'; never seen anythin' like this neck o' the woods, I reckon. Right, m' lads?" Wes was barely intelligible, but the brothers were aware that he was still defending them. He turned back to Ray and they resumed their incoherent babble.

The boys found a log and sat down to a feast of trout and crispy fried potatoes.

"How many did you catch, Granddad?" Craig asked, as C.I. joined them.

"Enough for everybody—and that goes for breakfast, too! Good thing I did, 'cause them two fellers never got a bite. Fer that matter, they never got their hooks in the water." He closed with a raucous chortle.

Quiet descended as the evening came. In the fading light, C.I. gazed across the stream. The boys saw him stiffen slightly as he seemed to spy something. Slowly, he raised an outstretched arm and aimed a gnarled finger toward the far bank.

"Be still!" he whispered.

Riveted to the log, the boys turned their heads slowly and looked.

Their eyes focused on a majestic bull elk, emerging from the forest and approaching the water directly across from them. As they watched in silence, he lowered his mighty antlered head to drink. Just behind him, the bushes parted to reveal his timid mate, head held high into the wind, warily guarding him from unseen enemies. Once the big male quenched his thirst, he assumed the role of sentinel while his mate drank.

"Lucky us boys're downwind," C.I. whispered softly. "They cain't get our scent! Biggest dang buck I've ever seen—and a rack to beat the blazes."

As quietly as they had appeared, the two elk gracefully slipped from view and were gone.

"This here's a waterin' hole! Prob'ly be more animals a-comin' down. They drink at dusk and dawn. Couldna picked a better campsite myself!"

As if in response, a vigorous new rustling came with the breeze across the stream. A big brown bear blundered recklessly into the river and began slurping noisily, obviously having no fear of predators.

The boys realized they were having a glimpse of something primordial— a rare look at a vanishing wilderness.

"Granddad! That bear's as big as the one that almost got us!" Craig croaked.

"No, it's not—nowhere near as big!" Mark insisted.

"Shush up, you two! Bears like to swim, y'know!" C.I. warned.

That shut them up in a hurry. They didn't care to provoke another attack like the one they had recently escaped from, thanks to Mike.

The bear satisfied his evening thirst and lumbered off. Through the evening, an almost steady string of smaller animals came down to drink. Soon it was too dark to see them, and the boys went looking for the marshmallows to roast over the embers of the campfire.

After Ray and Wes finally had dinner, some semblance of sobriety returned and they joined the boys and the older man around the campfire. Wes seemed to be conscious enough for Mark and Craig to venture a question or two.

"Did you know about the old homestead up there, Uncle Wes?"

"Yup. Some say that's the old Crampton place."

"What happened to them?" Craig asked.

"No one seems to know. Happened a lot around here. Folks homesteaded this wilderness, back in the 90s, before there were even roads. Then, they just picked up and left. Some say they just got sick of the rain!"

"They had a crab apple orchard," Mark offered.

"Yeah, we brought some!" Craig remembered, diving into his pockets. "Anyone want one?"

There were no takers.

"Speakin' of folks disappearin', Wes, what about them two hunters what got lost up here a while back?" C.I. asked.

"Not much to tell. They were wandering around the woods for a few days, looking for the way out. They stumbled onto Goodman about a mile up from here, and decided to follow it down to the coast to get back to civilization. When they reached this gravel bar right here, they saw the cliffs down there and knew they'd have to swim on down to the beach. They dumped their gear where we're sittin' and were never seen again. Folks figure the tide caught them, and they drowned against the rocks down there at the mouth, there bein' no beach," Wes concluded.

"You mean, they never found their bodies?" Mark asked.

"Not hide nor hair of 'em."

"Helluva hard country—not fer greenhorns!" C.I. remarked.

Mark and Craig slipped into their moss-cushioned sleeping bags with a new appreciation for this beautiful but menacing land. It offered so much yet was so unforgiving at the same time. A mistake in judgment could prove fatal.

The boisterous banter of the three men at the campfire made sleep impossible for the two brothers. Craig was turning over in frustration, peering toward them. Through the flickering flames he caught sight of Ray pulling something from the inside of his hunting jacket.

"Hey, Dad! Remember my navy chum, ol' Ab-Normal? And how I was just saying I never heard from him after Murmansk? Well, the damndest thing happened—I just got a letter from him—after eight years! And here it is!" he said, waving the envelope over the flames.

"Well I'll be dad-burned! Can you read in this light? I'm all ears!" C.I. said.

"Wes, you'll want to hear this, too. Pretty amazing stuff!" Ray squinted at the envelope. "It's been forwarded all over—went to the Navy Department first, then Great Lakes, even Portland—finally caught up with me after *four months!*"

9

February 5th, 1952
Dear Ray,

How's my old chum? Guess you must have wondered what happened to me over there in Mother Russia! I don't guess you'll call me friend after I say what I have to say.

A lot has happened to me, not much of it good, but it's time to come clean with you, since you were always there for me.

First, I've got to say that I wouldn't have made it without the stipend that goes along with the Medal of Honor, and I owe all that to you. Believe me, you'll want to take it all back after you finish this letter.

I must have started a hundred letters to you, but I never got the guts to go through with it. This time I think I can. I don't have any idea where you are, but maybe the navy in its infinite wisdom can find you. Here goes.

I won't go into the details, but I was a Nazi spy, right from the beginning. When I first met you at Great Lakes, I was already passing intelligence about the base to my contacts. One time, you even helped me deliver the goods, and never suspected a thing.

That's the exceptional thing about you, Ray—you were a true friend. You accepted anything I did without question.

When we got assigned to the Armed Guard, my Nazi cohorts were thrilled. They knew that I would be able to provide information on the movement, armament, and composition of any convoy to which I was assigned.

Which I did, explaining the higher losses on my convoys.

When you told me about your secret message, I knew I had to find a way to get on that convoy with you. You made it easy.

What wasn't supposed to happen, my ship wasn't supposed to be sunk. I learned much later that that torpedo was meant for your

126

ship. When it hit us, I was drunk out of my senses and locked in my cabin. My ship went down with all hands—except for me and one of my gunners—and I shot him so there wouldn't be any witnesses to my dereliction of duty.

By now—you're pretty bright, I recall—you're no doubt enjoying the ultimate irony: I used the German grenade I gave you to sink that "enemy" U-boat, and then you saw that I got a Medal of Honor for it! Still friends? Read on.

After the U-boat exploded and I fished you out of the drink, I saw my chance at your message. You were in such bad shape I had no trouble. The cigarette case was already sprung—so in nothing flat I memorized the code. Never did find out what it was all about, but like a good counterespionage agent I delivered it to my Nazi contact in Murmansk. Met her at the Red Star—and believe me, chum, Russian pussy was even better than I'd heard! But if that gorgeous gal I saw you with gave you any, you already know that.

You already know I missed the convoy—never dreamed we'd turn around that fast! That scared me some, since I knew I might be investigated. But your friend—the naval attaché—took care of me, per your instructions, and got me on the next convoy home.

He also told me about the Medal of Honor thing. And sure enough, it came through. Funny thing is, I'm proud of that medal—carry it on me everywhere I go. Even had my name engraved on the back.

Trouble is, my side lost the war. Not much of a future for an ex-Nazi spy in these United States! And worse yet, someone is after me. Probably it's the KGB—I had the feeling the Russkies were hot on my heels when I left Murmansk. I heard rumors through my contacts that whatever was in your message enraged Hitler, and he ordered the retreating German army to murder all Russian prisoners. Any way you look at it, I'm directly responsible for the deaths of countless thousands of human beings.

So, I've been on the run since the war ended. I haven't seen my wife and kids for years. I don't dare even tell them where I am. So far I seem to be keeping one step ahead of them, but it's a tough life. I've been hitting the bottle pretty hard. It's been seven years *now—I don't know how much longer I can keep running.*

I'm finding it harder and harder to live with myself because of what I've done. I knew what I was doing, I went in with my eyes wide open. I really thought the Nazis had the answer to a brave new world. Now I know better, but I also know there's nothing I can ever do, good friend, to right the wrongs I've done, or to heal the wounds I've opened in your soul.

The only thing I can be proud of in all this is that you are alive because of me. I am enclosing a souvenir of that momentous event.

Maybe I'll run into you sometime at the Copacabana, ol' chum!

Ab

The first time Ray had read the letter, he had gone into a furious rage. Vicky had thought how fortunate it was that the boys were gone. In time, as he reread it, his feelings changed. Now, tears glistening in his eyes, Ray tipped the envelope into his hand, and something fell out. He held it up to the dying firelight, and the men gazed in silent awe.

Reflecting redly in his fingers was the jagged U-boat fragment his traitorous friend had removed from his shoulder in the North Atlantic.

The sounds of the men carousing into the night became more and more unreal as Mark and Craig finally settled into an uneasy sleep.

10

Craig awoke to the *whirrrr* of a fishing reel and opened his eyes just in time to see his grandfather's hook and sinker make contact far out in the placid stream. He closed his eyes again, taking a deep breath, and savored the smell of bacon sizzling in a pan over the campfire. It was toasty warm inside his sleeping bag. But outside, the wet drizzle falling from the early morning sky had dampened the entire camp.

As awareness slowly crept back, Craig remembered the nightmare—he had dreamt about the hobo again! Those eyes that never closed—he always saw those eyes! Looking over at Mark, he wondered why he never saw them.

Mark was still sound asleep. Craig thought about waking him to tell him about the dream, but just then C.I. had a strike. Craig sat up to watch him reel in the first trout of the day—and it was a beauty!

The commotion rousted the rest of the camp. Moans and curses were heard from the direction of Ray and Wes, bedded down over among the rocks on a slight incline. The two men had mostly fallen out of their sleeping bags and were lying on the wet rocks, soaked and miserable from the rain, the unsatisfactory accommodations, and the previous night's excesses. Mark sat up and smelled the bacon.

"What's for breakfast? I'm famished!" he said through a stretch.

. . . . .

After an unusually quiet breakfast, they broke camp—Mark and Craig doing the lion's share—and were in the boat heading back down Goodman Creek before the sun had even risen above the trees. Wes was grumbling about their short stay. "Hellfire! We just got here!" He groused on about having to catch the outgoing tide, and he was in no shape to be a tour guide on the return trip. He grew ominously silent and morose as he piloted the little craft downstream.

Craig, too, had been quiet all morning, still not fully recovered from his haunted sleep. He was leaning over the side, gazing into the clear depths, as the boat glided swiftly through the canyon. Mark was watching him, wondering what was bothering his younger brother, when he saw Craig stiffen suddenly, his eyes widening in fear.

"Craig, what is it?" Mark yelled above the putt-putt of the outboard.

"I—it's—the eyes! I-it's—*his* eyes!" Craig's rasping words came out in a hoarse whisper. "There's a b-b-*body* down there!"

Mark, the hair rising on the back of his neck, looked where Craig was pointing as whatever it was slid astern.

"I see it, too! Uncle Wes, quick, turn around!"

"Too late, lads! Tide's got us—no way we can fight this current now!" Wes was suddenly stone-cold sober and intent on his navigating responsibilities.

The pale image faded as the boat and its occupants were lifted and then drawn downward toward the rocky seacoast.

"Goddamn kids and their wild fuckin' imaginations!" Ray sputtered furiously, his epithet lost in the tumultuous crashing of the waves on all sides.

Mark and Craig saw nothing but those eyes.

Sometime later, as the boat rode the waves back up the coast toward La Push, Wes looked with pity at the two violently sick boys, vomiting their guts out over the side. He thought, *Lads caught sight of one of those hunters, I reckon. What's left of him, anyway—poor devil!*

11

Dreary, gray rain clouds had settled over the mill camp. Several gloomy days of unrelenting rain only made the boys more despondent. The ground surrounding their grandparent's house was transformed into a bog, so saturated that walking on it produced a trail of small puddles. The brothers felt trapped in the little house, the unending, idle hours at first merely tedious, but in time making them face unwanted memories.

So, when their grandmother announced her weekly shopping trip into Forks, they leapt at the opportunity to escape from the doldrums of inactivity. The usually drab logging town loomed in their minds like the Emerald City of Oz on this dismal day.

Forks did not disappoint them. A break in the clouds produced a patch of blue sky that brought the sun out, and their spirits rose along with the steam floating up from the wet pavement. They saw Hattie bustling toward the car, emerging from the post office and cheerily waving a letter at them.

"A letter from your Mom, boys!" she sang out. The brothers grinned happily.

Mark snatched the envelope from his grandmother's grasp. "I get to read it first!" he said, tearing it open.

"Hurry up!" Craig complained.

Mark began reading, to himself.

Tuesday, June 24th
Dear Mark and Craig,

I'm really missing you guys. I hope you're having fun and finding lots to keep you busy up there. And I hope the weather is nice for you.

From what Dad said, it sounds like you had a wonderful camping trip down the coast. Sorry to hear you both got sick on the way back, though.

It sure is quiet around here without you two. Since Dad started his new job, Meg and I have hardly seen him. He goes to work early and comes home late. But other than the long hours, he seems happier than I've ever seen him.

Got a letter from Karl the other day, and he said to say "hi" to you guys. His job with the Bureau of Public Roads is way back in the Rogue River country of Oregon. He says the nearest town is thirty miles by wagon track, and since he's in charge of getting supplies, he has to drive it round trip twice a week in an old Ford pickup.

Last week I took Meg shopping, and she bought a cute summer outfit. She can't wait to show you. She says to tell you she's getting tired of doing all the dishes, so if you come home she'll bake you some cookies!

Last night at my Enatai meeting, Suzanne and I took the honors at bridge. I was tickled to get her as my partner since we're used to playing together, and winning seemed easy.

Meg and I aren't too lonely. We have Tito and the cats to keep us company, and it seems the hoboes haven't given up on us yet— one keeps showing up back by the playhouse. Nothing to worry about, though—he's not coming to the door.

Well, you boys take care of yourselves and don't get into any more mischief with bears! Hope you run out of steam pretty soon, and come home for a visit; we'll spend some time down the bay.

Love,
Mom

"C'mon, Mark! Lemme have it!" Craig yelled, tugging at the letter.

Mark, obviously unnerved by something their mother had written, held on tightly. Instead of handing it to Craig, he shoved it under his nose and, pointing to the distressing words, whispered, "Shhh!"

The word "hoboes" seemed to leap from the page, and Craig's protesting was over. Mark studied his brother's face as the meaning came clear. Craig turned, and their eyes met.

Their mother needed them again.

12

Sunshine returned with the Mosiers to the mill camp. Hattie knew the boys had been suffering from cabin fever.

"Go on—have some fun, you two! You been holed up long enough, with the rain and all. I'll take care of these groceries!"

Instinctively, the brothers headed for the mill, seeking shelter—even comfort—amid the screaming saws, the groaning chains and conveyors, the crackling fire, the pounding of the rhythmic steam engines. Losing themselves in the deafening cacophony had the startling effect of calming the turmoil in their minds.

Since they hadn't visited with their cousin Jed yet this trip, they decided to go there first.

This was one of their favorite parts of the mill. Jed was responsible for stoking the boilers that powered the mill—and the entire camp. This was accomplished by feeding the mill's waste products into a gargantuan furnace. The smaller pieces of wood, bark, and sawdust were carried from the saws to the furnace by a series of chain conveyors high overhead that would spill their contents down metal chutes directly into the furnace below. The larger chunks of wood mostly dropped off the conveyor and formed huge woodpiles on either side of the chute. The stoker would stand near the three-foot circular hole in the shiny steel decking that opened directly into the blazing inferno beneath his feet. Armed with a long pole fitted with a gaff hook, Jed would unerringly shoot these chunks of wood across the smooth deck and through the hole into the furnace. He was so adept at this that the boys would usually be treated to the sight of flames leaping high above the opening, sending sparks flying, heating the metal flooring so that it was too hot to touch.

"Hi, Jed!" Mark cried out, loud enough to be heard above the roaring furnace. Jed held out his right hand—er, hook—to shake hands, as was his way.

"Hey, Mark! Hey, Craig! Heard you guys were back. You came by just in time—take a look up there!" He pointed to the topmost conveyor. "I got me a real jam up there—Mark, think you can climb up and clear it for me?"

"Sure thing!" Mark grinned back. Where Jed had indicated, cedar bark and debris had clogged the conveyor chain. Material was backing up in the trough and beginning to spill over the side.

Craig, without a word, was already halfway up the woodpile leading to the conveyor.

Jed roared out, "Craig! Get down outta there! Ya little—!"

Mark scrambled furiously up the woodpile, after his little brother.

As Jed watched, Craig reached the catwalk that led along the furnace side of the conveyor. He bent over the trough and began pulling out some of the pieces. One particularly large chunk was jammed so tightly that Craig straddled the chute and pulled with all his might.

"Craig, NO!" Jed's voice boomed to no avail.

The piece suddenly gave way, and before Craig could get his balance, he fell over backward toward the chute leading to the insatiable flames below. With perfect timing, Mark launched himself into a flying block that knocked Craig away from the chute and landed them both roughly on the opposite side, sliding out of control down the woodpile. The boys lay in stunned silence on the steel floor, flames leaping up from the gaping hole beside them.

"You boys all right?" Jed huffed as he ran up to them. Then, he grumbled to himself, "I must be nuts gettin' kids to do a man's job!"

Jed assured himself that there was no harm done, then said gruffly, "Why don't you boys run along now—I've gotta catch up on my work!"

"Yeah. C'mon, Craig. Let's leave him alone. How about we go out on the pond?" Mark said.

"Okay, it's too hot in here anyway!" Craig wheezed. "'Bye, Jed!"

The huge quantities of cedar logs obscured the black, oily surface of the millpond. To Mark and Craig, it looked like a vast, undulating field of fallen trees. They loved to run across the pond, jumping quickly from log to log, putting enough of a spin on each log that when they reached the far side, all of them would still be rolling.

Craig, standing at the bottom of the bullchain, took a deep draft of the fresh air, looked across the pond to plan his route, and began his run.

Normally, the two brothers would be side by side. This time, Mark was caught off guard by Craig's sudden initiative. A moment's hesitation was his undoing, for it meant jumping onto logs already left spinning by Craig's flying feet.

Craig seemed to be filled with new life, and he skipped across the logs effortlessly. Ecstatic with his prowess, standing triumphantly on the other side of the pond, he turned to jeer at his older brother.

But Mark was nowhere to be seen. Instead, Craig saw two logs, spinning in opposite directions, their motion shooting a narrow column of oily froth high into the air.

Craig saw with horror that the logs were closing the gap where Mark had gone under. He began leaping logs two at a time, and when he reached the spot, he threw himself down, gripping one log for all he was worth, while pushing mightily with his small feet against the opposing logs. Slowly, almost imperceptibly, the logs moved apart.

At that moment, Mark's head bobbed up to the surface.

"Quick, Mark! Climb up! I can't hold 'em apart much longer!" Craig pleaded, in imminent danger of falling in himself. Mark spewed forth a fine spray of black froth and clawed blindly at the nearest log. He climbed out, coughing and choking.

A while later, the two brothers reclined on the bank, panting and looking at each other, then at the mill. They saw it now for what it really was: a screaming monster belching fire and smoke, ready to consume them at every turn. Its enchantment was over. They would not find comfort there again.

After a long time, Mark said, "You know, Craig, I think I've had enough of Forks for one summer. What if we ask Grandma to take us home?"

"Yeah," Craig quietly agreed. "I'm ready."

PART V

Craig inverted the envelope and tapped the contents into his open palm. Out fell a stiletto-like fragment of metal. He held it so Mark could see. The light from tiki torches mounted on the lanai railing reflected off the jagged surface as Craig turned it in his hand.

"My God, it's still here!" Craig said in wonder. "A piece of a U-boat sunk over half a century ago!"

"Let me see that thing!" Craig handed it to Mark, who examined it closely. "Wonder if ol' Ab's fingerprints are still on it!" he joked.

The moon was setting behind Kalihiwai Ridge, but the brothers did not notice, so engrossed were they in their travels back in time.

Casting aside the empty carton, Craig pulled over the last unopened box, wondering what treasures it might contain.

"My turn!" said Mark. He tore it open, reached in, and pulled out a hardbound book, its dust jacket still intact.

"'Hoboes of the Northern Pacific Railway,'" Mark read, "by Morton Jewell. Did you ever see this book, Craig?"

"No! So, all that research he did—with our help—he published a book, and we never even saw it?"

Mark opened the cover and gasped. "Holy shit, listen to this: 'Dedicated to Mark and Craig, who took care of Pay Day Paddy!'"

"He put that in the dedication? Is it a signed copy? See if he wrote an inscription," Craig ordered.

Mark flipped a page. "Yes! If I can make it out...here it is:

'To Ray: You will never know how much your sons have done for you!
Signed, Morton Jewell, 11 October 1954.'"

"Son of a bitch!" Craig hissed through clenched teeth.

1

Morning touched the tops of the trees on Water Street with gold. Craig stirred in his bed and raised himself on one elbow to look out the window at the scene below. It was going to be a sunny day!

The summer of 1952 brought big changes in the Mosier household. Since Ray had become lieutenant governor, the Mosier family fortunes had improved enough that they no longer needed the income from tenants.

They had expanded to fill the entire house, and Mark and Craig had moved two floors up. They now shared a huge sun-filled bedroom with polished hardwood floors and wood-panelled walls, in stark contrast to the dank concrete in The Dungeon far below. They also had twin beds, having left the bunk beds behind forever.

The upstairs consisted of a two-bedroom unit complete with its own living room, kitchen, and bathroom. The boys' bedroom was on the right at the top of the stairs, across from the bathroom. Straight ahead was the large living room, with fireplace, that became the master bedroom for Ray and Vicky. Through this room was what had been the tenant's kitchen, and then the second bedroom, which became Meg's. (Poor Meg—having to traipse through her parents' bedroom whenever coming or going! But she wasn't complaining, since she had moved from the tiny "sewing room" downstairs.)

Karl now had his own room at the back of the house, the apartment with its own outside entrance.

At this moment, Mark's thoughts were the same as Craig's. He stretched, and wondered what adventures might come their way on this halcyon summer's day.

Craig considered the possibilities. *We could go swimming at The Point. Maybe a few turns on the rope swing to start, to see if the weather will be warm enough.*

Or, we could climb the maple tree, Mark thought. He looked over to see if Craig was awake yet. Craig was looking at him wondering the same thing.

Craig began: "Let's go—"

"—on the rope swing!" Mark finished. They often had the same thought, so this coincidence did not strike either of them as being particularly unusual.

Whatever their plans, they would no doubt include their cousin Timmy, or one of their friends, maybe Don or Tippi.

They had learned long ago that if they wanted company, all they had to do was take a ride or two on the rope swing, and kids would show up.

This had helped Mark and Craig live with their awful memory of the midnight burial and the nearby grave. Each time they swung out into the air, the grim reminder was there, just off to the left. Alone, they were terribly conscious of it, but with friends around them they were usually able to put it out of their minds. Everyone wanted a turn, of course, and there were the inevitable accidents. Falling off the rope swing almost always resulted in serious injury.

The brothers bounded down the stairs, through the dining room, and into the kitchen. They raced to see who could get through breakfast first. Mark won, as usual, and was out the door as Craig stuffed the last of his toast and peanut butter into his mouth.

The woods were cool and dewy, and the early rays of sunlight filtered through the trees. Mark was completing his first swing when Craig arrived, still chewing.

"Yahoo!" Mark's cry of freedom echoed through the damp woods.

The familiar yell came faintly but distinctly to Tippi's ears, her summons to fun.

Tippi was the only girl in their circle of friends, probably because she lived only two houses away. She was a little older than Mark, dark and slender, and incredibly fleet of foot. She could outrun all the boys in the neighborhood, so she had earned their respect. She could also jump, whinny, and gallop just like a horse, which she often pretended to be. There was a loveliness about her, a nymphlike quality that fascinated the young boys.

Mark and Craig were always happy to see Tippi and loved to watch her lithe form swinging among the trees. They always let her have the most turns. Mark hated to admit it, but her prowess on the swing exceeded even his own.

Sometime later their curly headed cousin Timmy arrived. Stocky and brash, he was reckless and foolhardy on the swing, always having near-accidents and bragging that he was better on it than anybody else.

Tippi alighted from a particularly high swing with a flourish, and tossed her long hair, in exactly the way a filly tosses its mane. "Hey, you guys!

Wanna go swimming at The Point?" It was like a dare.

"I do!" was Craig's quick answer.

Everyone agreed it was a perfect day for a swim. And since they all had come prepared with bathing suits on under their clothes, the race was on. "Beatcha!" Tippi challenged, already with a big lead.

The boys all knew they couldn't catch Tippi, but they were pretty fast, too. Except for Timmy, who stumbled along until he tired and dropped out.

They ran up Water Street to the top of the trail, which led down a hogback steeply to a little point on the lake. Mark and Craig found Tippi already splashing in the cool water, taunting them for their tardiness. They wasted no time in joining her.

"Isn't Timmy coming?" Tippi asked.

Mark looked up the hill. "Guess not."

She dived under water and swam closer to the two brothers. Mark looked down and gestured to Craig: "She did it again—no suit!"

"Wow!" was all Craig could think of to say, sad that his glasses had been left safely behind on the bank.

As if by accident, as she had done once or twice before, she brushed gently against both boys' private parts just before surfacing.

Mark and Craig looked at each other in silent anticipation as Tippi slowly left the water. "Don't peek!" she said tantalizingly.

They drank in her supple nudity, but were too embarrassed to leave the water themselves for a little while.

The lake had gone from being a mysterious, distant, untouched object to an inviting, warm, inseparable part of their lives. It had revealed its secrets gradually over the years, in a process that was ordered according to the brothers' wishes.

Ever since that day when they first reached its shore, they had not been able to stay away. Each and every time they went into the woods they found themselves inexplicably drawn to it.

Adding to the enchantment of the lake was Mark's tale of a fabulous cavern extending far beneath its waters. The entrance was to remain always his secret, but the suggestion was that it was near the shore, possibly through a hollow stump. Craig was not let in on the secret, so he and their friends had searched for it in vain. Their curiosity grew with each new description of the cave's wonders: bejeweled chests overflowing with precious stones, walls that appeared to be lined in shimmering gold, a softly glowing light from some unknown source, and other surprises that Mark only hinted at. When asked why he couldn't reveal these treasures, Mark would become very serious and say that a terrible curse would be placed on him if he did. And, to heighten the mystery, there were those times when Mark seemed to disappear from the face of the earth. When he reappeared, he would always say that he'd been visiting his secret cavern.

But the realities of the lake drew them away from the fantasies of the cavern.

And they had discovered The Ship! This was the floating stump of an old tree whose trunk resembled the prow of a Viking longboat. Now the farthest shores of the lake were within their reach. The boundaries of their backyard world had grown beyond their wildest dreams.

2

One fine afternoon they were poling The Ship on an expedition to the north end of Capitol Lake. Joining Mark and Craig on this occasion was cousin Timmy.

Originally, The Ship would barely accommodate the two brothers, having a penchant to list precariously to starboard. But thanks to some expert modifications, another passenger or two could be added with marginal safety. Much of the center that had been the trunk was rotten and had been easily scooped out by the boys. Across this hollowed-out portion they had placed an old board for sitting, but the craft could not be propelled easily from there. Although it could be clumsily paddled, by far the best method of propulsion was by using the long pole. Of course, in order to do that, The Ship had to be close enough to shore for the pole to reach bottom.

Today's destination was one of their favorites: The Cliffs across the Northern Pacific Railway trestle. Since they loved walking across the trestle, they landed The Ship on the near side of the lake, climbed up to the tracks, and walked the rails to the other side. There was a railway spur that almost always had some sidelined flatcars and boxcars. These they would have to climb over or under to gain access to The Cliffs. Today was no exception.

At the far end of The Cliffs, in an area normally avoided by the boys, was the "hobo jungle." This time it was different, and Mark cast a fearful glance in that direction.

"What do you think, Craig? Shall we go over there?" he whispered quietly.

"Gee, Mark—I dunno...."

"We might be able to find somethin' out, if they'll talk to us," Mark suggested. "Nothin' to lose—let's go!"

Timmy was a little distance ahead and turned around impatiently. "What're you guys doin'? Let's go climb The Cliffs!"

Mark and Craig changed direction without a word to Timmy and headed toward the camp. Timmy, fuming and nagging, fell in beside them. As the three boys approached the transient enclave, they felt increasingly uneasy and out of place. After all, they were paying an uninvited visit to this community of outcasts. The faces that turned to them were mostly expressionless and unsmiling.

Craig's legs were shaking so badly he could barely stand. He whispered in his brother's ear, "Mark, let's get outta here!"

At that moment, he felt eyes boring into him, and he turned to see a man skulking in the shadows behind the others, peering at him intensely.

Pulling on Mark's belt, Craig gasped, "B-back there—th-that's the guy I saw walkin' around The Playhouse!"

Mark thought, *This was a big mistake!* He was about to call it all off when one of the men spoke.

"Well, looky here! Three sprouts from the other side of the tracks!"

This witty remark was greeted by loud guffaws from several of the itinerants within earshot. One added his own comment.

"That's a good one, Freight-train!"

"Just what can we do for you, sonny?" Freight-train addressed Mark, since he was the biggest and obviously the leader.

Mark wasn't sure what to say. "Uh—we come over here all the time to climb The Cliffs, and we always see you guys over here. We kinda wanted to see what your—camp—looked like." Mark felt like his heart was in his throat. The men's somber, penetrating eyes scrutinized him closely.

The second hobo growled, "It's called a jungle, and now you've seen it. SKEDADDLE!"

That was all it took. The boys turned tail and ran back toward the trestle. The Cliffs could wait for another day.

The boys were unaware that their hasty departure produced general hilarity throughout the camp.

Nor did they notice the skulking hobo break away and fall in a distance behind them.

. . . . .

Homeward bound on The Ship, Timmy fancied himself as the galley master. There he sat on the board, chastising Mark and Craig for their slow progress. "I knew this was a dumb idea. We coulda rode our bikes and been home a long time ago!"

146

"Tough, Timmy! If you don't like it, we can put you ashore right here!" Mark shot back.

Timmy let that pass. "So, you guys wanna do somethin' tonight?"

"Like what?"

"I know. Let's camp out in The Playhouse!" Timmy looked pleased with himself.

Mark and Craig exchanged a furtive glance.

"Nah. It's really messy, there isn't any room," Mark said.

"And it's so dark and dirty," Craig added.

"Chickens! Cluck-cluck-cluck!" Timmy taunted.

Something snapped. Mark's eyes glinted green as he dropped the pole and jumped on Timmy, who was Craig's age and about the same size. Mark took one of his arms and twisted it. "Take that back, you little punk!"

Timmy was not easily intimidated, but he didn't like the situation: the pole was afloat and they were drifting out from shore. "Okay, okay! You dropped the pole!"

Mark let go of Timmy's arm as Craig made a valiant attempt to retrieve the pole. He leaned out too far and fell in.

Timmy began to laugh uncontrollably, and the tension was broken.

When Craig resurfaced, he grabbed ahold of the pole and maneuvered the other end of it around to The Ship. "Grab it!" he sputtered.

Timmy reached for the pole. Mark looked around Timmy at Craig, and the brothers made their silent agreement. As Timmy gripped the pole, Craig, still in the water, jerked on his end as Mark pushed Timmy from behind. Timmy took a half somersault and landed on his back with a huge splash.

Now it was the brothers' turn to laugh uncontrollably.

Craig and Timmy clambered back aboard, Timmy looking downcast. Mark felt a little sorry for the trick they had played on him.

"Okay, Timmy. You win. We'll stay in The Playhouse."

3

They pulled The Ship up to its accustomed place on the shore below their house. Mark and Craig diverted from the main trail back.

"Where you goin'?" Timmy called, irritated that the two brothers always seemed to be going their own way, and did so without giving him a clue.

"To The Cavern!" Mark teased.

Timmy's momentary excitement was crushed when Craig said matter-of-factly, "To get a load of wood." Mark gave his brother a spoiled-sport look that promised future shoulder-poundings.

"Ah, geez, you guys always gotta do chores. I'll meet ya at the top."

"Not if you want to eat dinner with us," Mark warned.

Timmy sighed and reluctantly followed his cousins. "What a bunch of crap," he mumbled under his breath.

They approached a large, neatly stacked pile of wood that the brothers had sawed recently from a nearby alder. There was always a tree on the ground to supply fuel for the two insatiable fireplaces in the house above. And every time the boys were in the woods, they had to carry a load up, in addition to the daily trips they took for this purpose alone.

"Load me up, Craig," Mark ordered.

Since Mark was the stronger of the two, he carried the biggest load. Craig would then grab whatever he could and follow Mark up the hill. This time, Timmy watched Craig grab three pieces, and did the same, bringing up the rear.

Panting and puffing from the steep climb, Mark and Craig dumped their loads against the side of The Playhouse to wait for Timmy. Mark turned to see what had become of him as Craig sprawled to catch his breath. Craig's awkward position brought his eyes level with The Playhouse wall. He thought he saw something there he'd never noticed before and scrambled closer for a better look.

"Hey Mark, lookit this!"

Mark came over and the two boys examined some strange markings carved into the wood.

At that moment, Timmy came gasping up the hill, only one spindly piece of alder remaining cradled in his arms.

The three boys entered the kitchen door. There sat Ray and Vicky, and it was plain that they were already well into their evening ritual of drinking. The Mosier brothers knew from long experience that their father was to be avoided at these times. He became like a smoldering volcano waiting to erupt, explosive and unpredictable, and more dangerous with each drink. Tonight, because of Timmy and their plans, they had no choice but to face him.

"Don't you lazy shits ever do any goddamn work around here?" he ranted, eyes blazing. "You were supposed to mow the goddamn lawn today! Don't you ever do what the hell I tell you?"

Uh-oh, Mark thought. *We forgot to sickle the dandelion stalks after we mowed. We're in big trouble now!* The old push lawnmower did well enough on the grass, but it was too dull to cut the weeds that grew everywhere. Whenever they neglected this part of the job, Ray accused them of not mowing the lawn at all.

"But Dad, we—"

"Don't talk back, you worthless shits!" Ray bellowed, the veins standing out on his neck and forehead, right temple throbbing redly.

Ray was winding up to backhand Mark when he saw Timmy.

He grabbed his drink and stormed out of the kitchen, cursing under his breath.

Timmy whispered into Craig's ear, "Yer old man's a real bugger, ain't he!"

"Mom, the three of us are camping out in The Playhouse tonight. Can Timmy stay for dinner so he doesn't have to go all the way home and come back?" Craig asked timidly.

"Sure, honey. As long as he likes macaroni and cheese," Vicky said cheerfully, winking at Timmy.

"Yummm!" harmonized the boys.

Vicky realized Ray was far too hard on the boys and tried to make up for it in any way she could. Their father's habit was to control the boys by taking away their freedom. He robbed them of any sense of accomplishment by never being satisfied with the completion of a task and forced them to perform an endless repetition of drudgery.

"Don't worry about your Dad, boys. I'll get him all calmed down. And it'll help when I tell him you're finally putting The Playhouse to some good use!"

. . . . .

Vicky had joined Ray in the living room and the three boys sat at the kitchen table eating. Timmy had wolfed down his macaroni and was sitting impatiently. "Let's go!"

"Oh no!" It was Craig's muffled attempt to talk through a mouthful of noodles. "Isn't it our dish night?"

"You guys do dishes, too?" Timmy asked incredulously.

Mark ignored Timmy in answering Craig. "Nope. Meg's."

"Whew!" Craig sighed.

The evening was theirs.

4

In the months since that frightening moonless night, Mark and Craig had not so much as opened the door of The Playhouse. In fact, they had given it a wide berth whenever possible. And since Timmy had been with them all day, the brothers hadn't even been able to share their anxiety about what lay ahead of them this night. Not only had they avoided entering The Playhouse in broad daylight; now they were going to spend an entire night there. And its last nighttime resident had been a corpse!

The ancient flashlight threw its still-hesitant beam as the boys let Timmy take the lead. They held back as Timmy opened the door.

The sound of popping tendons reached out of the past and temporarily immobilized Mark. Craig, hanging on to Mark's belt, bumped into him, snapping him out of it. Then they were inside!

"Hey, this is neat! How come you guys've been keeping this place to yourselves?" Timmy loved it.

Mark and Craig busied themselves clearing space for three sleeping bags. Along two walls were waist-high benches that they put their dibs on, not wanting to be on that floor. To their relief, Timmy was content to spread his bag on the dusty planks beneath their feet, blissfully ignorant of past events.

As the darkness deepened, recurring images of the dead man haunted the brothers' vision. Shadows created by the flashlight's movement heightened the illusion.

"Hold it still, Timmy! I can't see what I'm doing," Mark snarled.

"Cool it, Mark! What's the matter with you guys, anyway! Scared?"

Quickly the boys climbed into the relative security of their sleeping bags.

Timmy said, "Alright, who tells the first ghost story?"

Silence.

"Well?"

"Let's just go to sleep," Craig yawned.

"Okay, I'll start. There's this guy and his girlfriend, see, parked in the woods, making out."

"Come off it, Timmy! We've heard this one," Mark ventured, fighting off his own ghost.

"The radio's on, playing music. The music stops and a guy's voice comes on, saying that this maniac killer just escaped from the insane asylum. He describes the crazy guy, and he's got this hook instead of an arm. Things were getting pretty hot between the guy and his girl until then. But the girl freaks out and says she wants to go home. So the guy's mad, see, and he peels outta there." Timmy paused for effect.

Forced to listen, the brothers were spellbound, hearts pounding in their ears.

"The guy really lays rubber. He's so mad he just wants to dump her. But when he gets to her house he remembers her door sticks and has to be yanked open from the outside. So he gets out and goes around to open it. That's when he finds it."

Another lengthy silence. Craig's curiosity won out over his fear. "Finds wh-what?"

"The hook—the hook arm—it was hanging from her door handle!" Timmy finished triumphantly.

Mark was glad to have it over with. "Like I said, Timmy—we already heard that one," he lied. It was common practice whenever the boys camped out to demean each other's storytelling abilities and to challenge each other to go one better.

"Yeah? You think you can tell a better one?" Timmy taunted.

Mark thought. *Why not? Timmy never believes any of our stories anyway.* He wished he could ask Craig what he thought.

"How about something that really happened?" Mark said. "Right here in The Playhouse!"

"Mark! No!" Craig protested.

"Shut up, stupid! I know what I'm doing."

Now Craig considered. *Maybe it's okay. Timmy will think it's all made up. Maybe it'll feel better to talk about it, but still....*

"There was this hobo..." Mark began. With considerable skill, he crafted a factual yet superbly embellished tale of The Hobo's demise.

The quiet inside The Playhouse could be cut with a knife. Timmy and Craig were both captivated by Mark's tale, each for his own private reasons.

"...and I put the body in The Cavern!" Mark finished, pleased with his ending twist.

The silence was short-lived as Timmy saw the flaw. "What a bunch of crap! Everyone knows there's no Cavern! You made up the whole thing." Timmy would never admit it, but in truth he had hung on every word.

Mark could tell from Timmy's outburst that he had told the better story.

To Craig, the retelling had been so vivid that he had closed his eyes and kept them tightly shut for the duration. Only after silence had closed in once more did he venture to open them. Lying on his back and peering upward through the blackness, he saw *the eyes* looking back at him.

No! It can't be! Craig's blood ran cold.

Eyes shut tight again, he prayed. *Please, God! Make them go away!* Summoning his courage, Craig made himself open his eyes to narrow slits.

The eyes above him were still there: cruel, penetrating, *staring vacantly*.

Craig was emitting short, rasping breaths. Timmy complained, "Hey, who's makin' noise now? Aren't you guys ever goin' to sleep?"

"What's the matter, Craig? Another nightmare?" Mark asked with concern.

Utter terror in his voice, Craig said, "Th-those eyes—*his* eyes—th-they're staring at me again! Up there!"

Mark switched on the dim flashlight and pointed its beam at the ceiling.

"It's just those eyes that Karl painted up there, stupid! The ones that glow in the dark!"

The weak light revealed a pair of rudely painted luminous eyes on the overhead beam.

Timmy's unabated giggling went on into the night and made Craig feel increasingly foolish. But—just to be safe—he kept his eyes closed.

. . . . .

"What's this?" Timmy was asking.

The early morning light had transformed the interior of The Playhouse into something more familiar, almost friendly. Mark opened his eyes and focused on something Timmy was waving in his face.

"The Hobo's hat!" Mark blurted, before he realized what he was saying. Timmy's face registered shock.

It was beyond coincidence. Mark and Craig hadn't thought of The Hobo's hat in all this time—and *now*, their loudmouth cousin held it in his grasp.

"You guys set me up! You planted this here, didn't ya?" Timmy snorted, disdainfully throwing the hat into a corner.

"You'll never know," Craig said bitingly, still smarting from his cousin's ridicule of the night before.

"Oh yeah? What a bunch of crap!"

Having Timmy right where they wanted him, the brothers let it go. They gloated momentarily as they realized that "The Story of the Hobo" would remain fiction as far as Timmy was concerned.

Later on Mark returned to retrieve the hat and put it where he thought no one would ever find it.

5

Morton Jewell had been a tank commander in the Allied invasion of Germany. Born and raised in Olympia, he had been a schoolmate of Vicky's. He and Ray had become good friends during the last year of the war in Portland, where they had met by coincidence. After a brief try at civilian life, he reenlisted to serve in occupied Germany. Now he had left the service and was returning to Olympia to resume his interrupted writing career.

Vicky had also become close friends with Morton's wife, Ruby, while both families were in Portland. Now the little two-bedroom bungalow next door had come available, and it was perfect for the Jewells and their two young daughters.

While in Portland, Ray had told Morton the story of his exploits on that fateful Run to Murmansk, and it had inspired Morton to write a book documenting the war in the North Atlantic. The book, *S.O.S. North Atlantic*, had since been published, and Ray relished the lengthy chapter devoted entirely to his—and Ab's—heroic feats.

Morton was a large, well-built man, standing six-feet-two, with a handsome, distinguished face, and a rich, deep voice whose mellow tones commanded authority. His imposing manner was a facade that he dropped whenever Mark and Craig were around. He treated the brothers like the sons that he never had. Mark and Craig delighted in this affection, perhaps because they never received it from their own father.

· · · · ·

The October day dawned dark and rainy. But the Mosier brothers' spirits were not dampened by the gloomy weather, for today they were going to Westport with Morton—and their Dad, unfortunately—to see if they could dig their limit of razor clams.

Their father was behind the wheel of his brand new 1952 Plymouth, bragging about it and his new lease on life. "Nice car, eh Mort? First new car I've bought since Vicky and I got married. Damn near doubled my salary when the governor appointed me."

"Exceptionally fine motorcar if I do say so, Mr. Lieutenant Governor, sir!"

Sitting in the back seat of the car, there wasn't much for Mark and Craig to do but listen to the two men's conversation up front. The sound of the tires hissing on the wet concrete, the rain pelting against the windshield, and the noisy rhythm of the wipers made even this a difficult endeavor. It appeared to the boys that their dad was in a good mood today, so they hoped for the best.

"So, what're you working on now, Mort?" Ray asked his friend.

"You know me. I need something to stir up my curiosity, like you did with your Armed Guard story."

"That's one helluva book. Especially chapter five!" Ray grinned.

Morton noted the compliment and continued. "Well, since we moved back to Olympia, I've noticed a queer thing going on around town."

"Yeah? What's that?"

"There seem to be more hoboes around than one would expect—especially now, seven years after the war. They even come to my back door, offering to work in exchange for food. Have you had any such visitors?"

"How the hell would I know—I'm always down at the State house! I don't work at home like some lucky bastards!"

"Has Vicky ever mentioned it?" Morton persisted.

Ray had never even thought about it. Thinking about it now, he said, rather annoyed, "She'd sure as hell tell me if she was being bothered by a bunch of bums!"

"I've already done a little research, my friend. And I must take exception with you there. Hoboes are *not* bums! A hobo is someone who *travels and works*. On the other hand, a bum doesn't travel *or* work. And the ones coming to *my* door are *hoboes*."

Ray shrugged this off indifferently. He couldn't care less about such subtle distinctions—they all looked like bums to him.

"Gimme a beer, Mort!"

In the back seat, Mark and Craig were staring wild-eyed at each other. This was an unexpected development. On the one hand, they were horrified to hear that their neighbor was checking on the movement of hoboes in Olympia—this might result in their father finding out that Vicky had indeed been feeding them—or worse! On the other hand, Mort might be able to help them figure out why the hoboes kept coming to their house. But could they trust him?

As the car raced on through the downpour, the boys' minds were racing as well, considering the wealth of possibilities now open to them. They both knew, no matter what the risk, that they would have to approach Morton when the time was right.

. . . . .

It was low tide when they arrived at the beach near Westport. Rain was still falling steadily and heavy fog made for zero visibility.

"Perfect weather for clamming!" Morton observed.

"Don't believe I've ever seen the sun shine down here," Ray agreed. "Think I'll just drive right down close, so we don't have to walk so far."

He guided his precious new car cautiously off the roadway and drove out onto the gray, hard-packed sand. The tires made instant dry spots as they passed over the wet sand, pushing the water away from the tread, filling in the moment they rolled on. The best clamming area was about a half mile out on the beach, in an area that would be under probably six feet of water at high tide. Ray drove out as far as he dared.

"What do you think of this spot, Mort?"

"You may be out a bit too far, chum. We'll have to keep an eye out when the tide turns."

Razor clamming wasn't at all like digging for the rock clams on the shores of Puget Sound. It required special techniques, employing a long, tapered shovel.

Mark was particularly skilled at this, and he set about the task with relish. He would look for the telltale sign of the clam's neck protruding from its hole in the sand, feeding on the nutrients found in the shallow water. He tread very lightly as he approached his first quarry. Drawing alongside, he squatted down and slapped his shovel on the wet sand next to the clam. In a flash, the neck withdrew into the hole, Mark took two quick scoops of sand, and thrust his hand down the hole. His whole arm disappeared from view, and he cried, "I've got it!" Then the fun began.

He grunted and groaned while he pulled with all his might. Finally, after what seemed a long time, a loud sucking noise could be heard as Mark began to get the better of the stubborn clam. Suddenly, with a jerk, he pulled free with his prize: a whopping eight-incher, its digger still working in a futile effort to escape.

The procedure Mark followed was a tried and true method of "catching" the elusive razor clam. He slapped the sand to make the clam withdraw its neck into its shell, thus preventing severing the juicy morsel with the sharp-edged shovel. With the slap, the clam would simultaneously begin its furious digging, and the "hunter" had to be fast enough to keep up with its incredibly rapid descent. He dare not take more than two scoops of sand, or he would risk crushing the razor-sharp shell. If this happened, he would receive deep lacerations as he reached blindly into the hole to grip the clam.

The ordeal was so difficult that few attained the limit of twelve clams per person. Today's catch totaled thirty by the time Ray noticed the water lapping at the Plymouth's tires. Closer inspection revealed that the tires had settled slightly into the sand.

"All right, everyone! Let's pack it in—water's risin'!" Ray yelled anxiously.

They hurriedly loaded their buckets and shovels into the trunk and got in. Ray started the engine, put it in low gear, and let out the clutch. The car made a little lurch and stalled.

"What the shit—!" Ray swore. He tried again, with the same result.

"Try second gear—we'll get out and push. Come on, boys!" Morton said.

Countless efforts failed to free the car. They tried rocking it back and forth, putting planks under the tires, but all to no avail. At length, a winded Morton walked around to the driver's side window, which Ray had rolled down partway.

"I'm afraid she's goin' down, Ray! Better get out and have a look."

As Ray opened his door, it skidded across the sand and stuck about halfway open. The tires had almost sunk from view! As Ray climbed out, the vehicle shuddered and began sinking slowly, steadily downward into the saturated sand. As he watched his prized possession being consumed before him, a needle of piercing pain began over his right temple. Clear thought was no longer possible, and he was gripped by a violent urge to lash out.

This time, because Mark was the closest, he took the full brunt of Ray's mindless fury. Ray's entire body flexed as he wound up to kick. The wild, powerful blow was totally unexpected and caught Mark squarely in the lower abdomen. Knives of excruciating pain doubled him up. He collapsed in a stunned heap on the wet sand.

"You fuckin' worthless turds! I'll kick the shit outta you!" He was in a shrieking rage. He turned toward little Craig, who cringed and prepared for the worst.

Morton was thunderstruck. He had never seen this side of Ray. He inserted his large frame between Ray and Craig, and grabbed Ray's arms. As he did so, Ray collapsed onto the sand, where he assumed the fetal position, holding his head and moaning.

Craig ran to Mark, who was grimacing in agony, gasping for air, and only semiconscious. Waves of pain swept over him.

As Craig knelt by his side, Mark recovered enough to grunt out, "It—it hurts real bad, Craig!"

With Craig's help, Mark was barely able to stand. Each step was excruciating, and he walked bent over, with his right hand pressing on his abdomen.

As Craig supported his big brother, he turned to watch the doomed car settling ever deeper into the sand.

. . . . .

The stranded clam diggers had hitched a ride to a cafe in Westport. Weary and bedraggled, and having lost the beer with the car, Ray and Morton were warming themselves over coffee while the boys had hot chocolate. Ray was pale and withdrawn, his hands shaking as he lifted his cup to drink. He did not look at his sons.

Mark suffered in silent pain. A bruise the size of a football was already forming where Ray had kicked him.

Mort had called Ruby, who was on her way with Vicky to pick them up. He was questioning Ray about his senseless outburst.

"Never saw you pull a stunt like that! Why'd you do it?"

"Well, you saw me lose the car—what do you expect?" Ray grumbled.

"But why take it out on your boys?"

"It's these goddamn headaches—I black out. I don't know what I'm doing."

"How long has this been going on?" Morton pursued.

"Hell, ever since the war, I guess."

"Ever talked to a doctor about it?"

"Doctors cost money, Mort. Never had that much to spare."

"Well, you do now, chum; old habits die hard. You're going even if I have to take you myself! Let's get you checked out. Who knows, you may have had a head injury they never found. After all, a U-boat did blow up in your face!"

Craig, listening intently, felt a glimmer of hope. Morton was the first outsider to witness one of their father's attacks. A man of rare courage, he had dared to confront Ray with it.

Mark absorbed little; all was hazy and surreal—pain was his only reality. Even so, he was dimly aware that Morton somehow held a key.

6

Mark's stomach pains had not improved. Vicky had taken him several times for tests, and each time the doctor had assured her it was merely "gas pains." They even took blood counts; always Mark went home with a clean bill of health. When the doctor asked him about the ghastly mottled bruise, Mark lied and said that he had taken a bad fall down the hill with an armload of firewood.

But the dull, persistent pain just wouldn't go away.

Mark's eating habits had changed drastically, and this worried his mother. It was not like him to leave food on his plate; usually, he asked for more than she had fixed, especially at dinnertime. Vicky was alarmed when Mark began to lose weight and could no longer keep his food down.

And, there was something else different now. He always seemed to walk stooped over, wincing in pain whenever he tried to stand erect.

Why couldn't the doctors find anything wrong? Vicky was puzzled.

. . . . .

Mark's earsplitting scream of agony shook the old house to its rafters, shattering the calm autumn night.

Vicky fairly streaked to Mark's bedside. There she found Craig, standing wide-eyed and helpless at Mark's side.

"Honey—what's wrong?" she asked, gently cradling Mark in her arms.

Mark was catching short breaths through clenched teeth and couldn't answer. He was deathly white.

"He's holding his stomach again, Mom!" Craig offered.

"Yes, dear, I can see that. Craig, why don't you go back to bed? Mark's going to be fine."

"Mom, I've never heard Mark scream like that in my life. Shouldn't we take him to the hospital?" Craig was dubious about putting this off.

"In the morning, honey. I'll sit with him for awhile."

161

Craig was always upset when Mark was hurting and climbed into his bed as tears began to flow. "It's...okay, Mark...."

. . . . .

Incredibly, the doctors were still stymied, and that's all it took for Ray Mosier. He mumbled something about this being another ploy to get out of school. "Bet he won't want to miss our trip to Mount Rainier this Saturday!" he said out loud.

Mark heard his father. A bitter pang was added to the pain that refused to let go of his abdomen. It wasn't fair, because he liked school and never played hooky. But of course, even in great pain as he was, he would not have missed an outing to their favorite mountain. So his father was right in his perverted way.

This meant that Mark had to act like he felt better, even though of course he didn't. He spent an agonizing Friday trying to look normal. Craig knew he was faking. Karl and Meg suspected it, too, but said nothing.

"C'mon, Mark, maybe we shouldn't go!" Craig was genuinely worried about his brother.

"We're goin'," he said remorsefully. "If I stay home, no one would get to go. We're gonna go!"

. . . . .

The trip to Mount Rainier was pure misery for Mark; in fact, it wasn't much fun for anybody. Even the weather was bad; it was cold and misty, and the Mosiers never did get a glimpse of the great snowcapped peak. The long ride over bumpy roads had not been good for Mark, and on their return he looked deathly pale.

Vicky was now more convinced than ever that something was very wrong.

"First thing Monday I'm going to raise a real ruckus with the doctor," Vicky said to her husband. "We've had him in four times, and they still don't know anything!"

"You mean he's gonna miss school again?" Ray grumbled.

"Well, just look at him! He's white as a ghost! I'm not letting him go to school until we get to the bottom of this!"

Vicky did not often take such a strong stand. Ray did not try to argue when she used that tone.

. . . . .

At Vicky's insistence, Mark's doctor took a fifth blood count, but he sent them away with the now-familiar promise: "We'll call you if we find anything unusual."

Vicky felt helpless. She was angry and frustrated, but she couldn't take it out on the doctor. *Modern medical science is pretty worthless,* she thought. *How sick do you have to be before they can do something?*

It seemed to Vicky that her son was slipping fast. Why was she the only one who seemed to care?

. . . . .

It was unusually quiet around the dinner table. Mark couldn't bear to even look at the food on his plate. Vicky apparently believed that as long as one could eat, everything was fine, so she stubbornly continued to coax him into eating.

The telephone shattered the silence. Vicky jumped up frantically. Maybe there was news at last!

"Hello?" she said anxiously.

"Mrs. Mosier? This is Dr. Scott. *Do not* let Mark eat anything! Bring him to the hospital *now*—he has a burst appendix! We have to operate right away. If he eats anything, it could kill him!"

Dropping the phone in a panic, she found her purse and ran toward the kitchen, shouting: "Ray! Help Mark out to the car while I back it out! We're going to the hospital! They have to operate! Quick!"

"Whhhaaat?" was Ray's startled reaction. He looked at his large son, then turned to Craig and said, "Come on! You heard your mother—give me a hand!"

At this point, Mark scarcely knew what was happening. He was vaguely aware of being transported at breakneck speed through the streets of Olympia and knew the destination was the hospital at the top of the steep hill across town.

Then, somehow, he was flat on his back in a strange room with blinding lights, shadowy figures looming around him, flashes of cold stainless steel reflecting nearby. The familiar voice of his doctor seemed to come to him on a beam of light.

"You're going to be all right, Mark. But I need your help. Can you count

163

backward for me? Starting from 100."

Mark really had to concentrate. "One hundred…ninety-nine…." And that was it.

"Scalpel!" was the last word Mark heard.

Dimly, fading fast, the last thing he saw was the glint of the razor-sharp steel making its descent.

. . . . .

"Mark's appendix ruptured at least four days before we operated. I've never seen a case like this. I really think the fall he took precipitated the rupture," Dr. Scott began.

Vicky absorbed every word with rapt attention. Ray shifted uncomfortably and averted his eyes.

"Normally, the poison is released into the system right away and can be detected by a blood test. In Mark's case, his system formed a remarkable abscess that contained the poison and kept it from being released into the bloodstream. That's why we couldn't detect it. If we hadn't operated today, the abscess would have burst, and the poison would have spread through his whole body. I doubt we could have saved him. Even now, there's a lot of poison there, and that's why we've left a tube—so that it will be able to drain out. And to ward off infection, we need to give him penicillin shots every four hours. All of this will take time. You'd better plan on leaving him here for a couple of weeks at least."

"Guess he wasn't faking it after all," Ray said. It was the closest he would ever come to admitting his guilt.

"We almost lost him—the big lug!" cried Vicky. Her term of endearment for Mark, used on this occasion, unleashed a stream of tears that soaked Ray's old shoulder wound where she leaned for support.

7

Billy Stolski hadn't improved with age. He was the biggest kid in the seventh grade. Except, of course, for Mark, who had grown an incredible nine inches over the past year, and now towered above his classmates at a height of nearly six feet.

Billy picked on all the younger, smaller kids. He had rarely been a menace to Craig before, because Mark was almost always nearby. On several occasions, Mark had stepped in and stopped Billy's abuse of those too small to defend themselves.

Billy hated Mark, but knew enough to steer clear of him.

But now Mark was in the hospital, and everyone knew it. Billy now had a free rein. It was not surprising that he set his sights on Craig.

In the past, Craig had always looked forward to recess. Now, when that bell rang, it filled him with dread. No sooner would he get out than Billy would be on him. Craig could outrun him, but Billy would lie in wait and take him down whenever he could. Then he'd sit atop poor Craig for the rest of recess, taunting him, poking him in the chest, slapping his face, humiliating him. "Give?" he would say, or "Say uncle!" Then, saved by the bell, Craig would find himself suddenly free. But Billy would give him a parting shot, and with a shove, once again sending Craig sprawling into the dirt, would say, "I'll finish the job later, you little creep!"

Craig liked to think he was brave and courageous. He knew he'd lose his self-respect if he complained to anyone about Billy. He didn't like kids who whined about their troubles.

So, he kept it all to himself.

. . . . .

It was Mark's first day back. He was under strict doctor's orders: no running, no jumping, no sudden movements, no bike riding—no fun! But this was fine with Mark, who with every move was painfully reminded of the eighteen stitches in his side.

Billy, unaware of Mark's return, lay in wait for his customary target.

"Bull's-eye!" he grunted, as he jumped out from hiding and hit Craig in a flying tackle.

Craig assumed his familiar position, face down in the dirt, and Billy was upon him, meaner than ever, jerking Craig over on his back.

Mark walked slowly out onto the playground. A classmate ran up to him, breathless. "Hey, Mark! Craig's gettin' beat up!" He pointed across the field, and Mark's pain was gone.

"STOLSKI!" He spat it out like an epithet.

. . . . .

"Where's your big tough brother now—huh, creep? You think he's so great, where is he when you need him? This one's for him!" The flat of his chubby hand slammed into Craig's cheek.

Billy gripped Craig by his shirt and pulled his face inches from his own. "Know what your problem is?" he sneered. "The best part of you dribbled down your mommy's leg!"

Craig winced as he saw Billy making a fist and winding up.

Billy's fist hung in midair. Craig, eyes shut tight, waited for the inevitable.

No blow came. Craig opened his eyes and was aware of a huge shadow looming overhead. It was Mark!

Craig saw the shocked look on Billy's face and felt the pressure suddenly lift off his chest as Billy became airborne. Holding the bully aloft with his left hand, Mark took aim and fired with the right, never letting go. The fist made contact with the point of Billy's chin, and Craig heard the crunch as the jawbone shattered.

Calmly, deliberately, Mark lowered the senseless boy to the ground, where he lay, slack-jawed and still.

Mark stood dazed over Craig, with eyes unfocused, weaving from side to side, face turning pale.

"Mark! Your stitches!" Craig cried.

Mark looked down at his waist numbly. His shirt was soaked with blood, and through a fog he realized that his wound had torn open, stitches ripped away.

The ambulance had two occupants that day.

. . . . .

Mark's second set of stitches was history when Billy Stolski finally returned to school. No longer the schoolyard bully, he was the subject of ridicule among his former victims. It was the cruel justice of his peers. With his jaw wired together, he was laughed at and taunted. For the first time, he experienced the humiliation he had once brought on others. Before long, he moved away.

Among their friends and classmates, Mark and Craig had gained notoriety. Mark's protective services had become legendary, and the playground was once again a fun place for all.

8

Mark and Craig were at the kitchen sink doing the dinner dishes. As much as the boys detested this chore, it was their only consistent source of income. Although they were required to perform this task three times a week, they *did* receive compensation: their mother would give them each a dime per wash. With this money, they had enough to attend the Saturday matinee, one of the highlights of their week; ten cents for the movie, ten cents for popcorn, and a nickel each for Coke and candy bar.

The brothers would become quickly bored with this mundane labor; besides, they thought it was unfair that they had to do household chores in addition to all the outside work. What were girls for, anyway? So, they would find innovative ways to make things more interesting.

Since Craig was a slow, methodical washer, Mark always had time for mischief. One of his favorite tricks was to rummage around in the tin table drawer for rubber bands to shoot at Craig. He would place himself strategically at the far end of the table, just out of range of splashing dishwater, and let fly.

There was a problem here. After drying his father's set of prized navy glasses, Mark would place them on the tin table for putting away later. Every now and then, one of these would fall victim to an errant rubber projectile.

Mark took careful aim at the back of Craig's head. The less than aerodynamic missile caught the rim of one of the fragile glasses and set it to wobbling precariously on the edge of the table. Craig heard the unsteady clattering, spun around just in time to see the glass falling, and made a spectacular diving catch. Unfortunately, he couldn't check his forward momentum, and he crashed into the leg of the tin table, sending two more unwary glasses tumbling to their inevitable fate on the floor below. The horrible crash of shattering crystal shot through the boys' hearts as if they had been pierced by the shards of glass themselves. They heard the sound echo through the kitchen and down the hallway.

Paralysis gripped the boys. Holding their breath, they knew all too well what would follow: the approaching sound of their raging father.

Thump-thump-thump-thump! The thunder of Ray's furious footfalls reached the boys' ears like the roar of cannon fire. The old house shook to its very foundations.

With the worsening of their father's physical attacks, Mark and Craig now lived in mortal fear of his insane reprisals. They looked at each other and instantly saw escape as their only hope. They were up and scrambling for the kitchen door as Ray made his shrieking entrance. Mark managed to jerk the door open in time to get away, but it was too late for Craig.

Charging through the door, Ray caught Craig a glancing blow to the back of the head and then tripped over the stand containing the croquet mallets. He lost his balance and went careening headlong down the back porch steps. His head smashed into the side of the garage with a loud thud, and he dropped limply to the ground.

Running around the back of the house, Mark let Craig catch up.

"You okay, Craig? C'mon, we gotta hide somewhere!"

"I think so," Craig panted, looking back to see if their father was pursuing them. "Mark, wait—he's lying on the ground back there! Let's go back and see if—"

"Are you nuts, Craig? We can't go back there. We'll get blamed—this time, he'll kill us!"

"I don't care, I'm goin' back!" Craig said decisively. Then, "Mark! C'mere, he's bleeding! We better tell Mom!"

Mark ran to join Craig and looked down apprehensively at his father's prone figure. He shook his head in disbelief. *Now what do we do?* he thought hopelessly.

Vicky suddenly appeared at the back door. "What's all the fuss—oh, my God!" she cried, hurrying down to Ray's side. "Ray? Ray!" She tried frantically to get him to respond, to no avail.

Vicky took charge, directing Mark to call for an ambulance and sending Craig for towels and a pillow for Ray's head.

. . . . .

"Your husband is very lucky, Mrs. Mosier," the staff neurologist was saying. "His concussion is not life-threatening. He should regain his faculties by morning. We don't think there'll be any lasting effects from this injury.

169

However—" he paused, frowning, reluctant to proceed.

"Yes—what is it, doctor?" Vicky prodded worriedly.

"The x-ray revealed something else. We can't tell exactly what it is, but there's a long, metal fragment—what looks like a needle about three inches in length—imbedded deeply into your husband's skull."

Vicky gasped. "Th-the war—he was wounded in an explosion. C-could it be shrapnel?"

"Possibly—odd shape for shrapnel, though. But whatever it's from, we can see that it's moving deeper—toward the brain."

"What would happen if it—" Vicky broke off.

"It could mean a number of things—disability, paralysis—even death."

"Is there anything we can do about it?"

The doctor was ready for this inevitable question. "We have two options. Leave it alone—and use medication if problems develop—or take it out. Either option has its risks to your husband."

"Problems already have developed. He has terrible, blinding headaches that throw him into a rage. He's already hurt our kids—I'm scared to death he'll do something worse. Let's get it out!" Vicky blurted.

"I'm afraid it's not that easy, Mrs. Mosier. We definitely don't have the facilities to do it here in Olympia. But there is a fine medical facility in Seattle, with some of the best brain surgeons in the country. Still, it *is* delicate surgery; I don't know of many operations of its kind having been performed. Of course, there is a plus side to that: all the best neurosurgeons will want to participate. I'll look into it for you if you like. But what about Mr. Mosier? Do you think he will agree? It'll put him out of action for about three months."

"I don't really know—he's so busy as lieutenant governor, and he *does* want to be governor. Besides, he *hates* hospitals! I guess all we can do is try to convince him—will you help me, doctor?"

"Of course, Mrs. Mosier—that's an important part of my job. But it still has to be his decision—and his alone," the doctor concluded.

Vicky was astounded when Ray almost eagerly agreed to the delicate procedure. She hadn't really been aware of the extent of his pain and the agony of the behavior it produced.

Within a week he had recovered sufficiently from his concussion to be transferred to King County Medical Center in Seattle. He was put under the care of a team of neurosurgeons, and the high-risk operation was successfully performed a few days later.

. . . . .

The light glinted off a long, thin sliver of metal in Vicky's fingers. "Is this it?" she asked.

Vicky was only able to get away one day a week for the sixty-mile trip to visit Ray in the Seattle hospital. It was on the third of these visits that Ray had recovered sufficiently to show some curiosity about the events leading to his operation.

"Yep, doctor just handed it to me this morning. One more piece of that U-boat—hopefully the last—for my collection! But what I don't understand is how they found it. Last thing I remember, we were having a drink in the living room. What happened then?"

"Are you really up to hearing this, honey?"

"'Damn the torpedoes—full speed ahead!'" Ray quipped, repeating one of his favorite quotes.

Vicky was encouraged by this lighthearted response, and grinned broadly. "Okay, here goes. The boys broke a glass in the kitchen, and you took off after them. I guess they ran out the kitchen door, because you fell down the back steps and smashed into the side of the garage. When I got to you, there were croquet mallets all over the place, so you must have tripped over the rack. In fact, I had to throw one mallet away—it was broken into pieces," Vicky lied in conclusion.

"How did I land in the hospital?" Ray queried.

"You were out cold, so we had to call an ambulance. It turned out to be a bad concussion."

"So how did they find that needle in my head?"

"You know, they've started to x-ray anyone with serious head injuries—and it showed up on the x-ray."

"I'll be damned. After all this time! It's like a big pressure has been lifted off my head—like—loosening a vise." He opened his arms to Vicky in a sudden emotional gesture.

Vicky came into Ray's arms, tears welling in her eyes, as the hope of a new life rose in her breast.

"Welcome back, sweetheart," she murmured softly.

Mark and Craig did not attach much significance to the operation until many years later. They were just elated for the freedom. They had been given a lengthy reprieve—nearly three months!—while their father was hospitalized.

9

Visiting Morton's house next door was a great treat for the Mosier brothers. They would usually find him in his study, wearing a smoking jacket and puffing on his Meerschaum pipe, clacking away at the old Underwood. The walls were decorated with antique flintlock and percussion cap pistols. Morton had a large collection of memorabilia, which he generously allowed the boys to paw over. Craig loved to don the Nazi Luftwaffe uniform and old spiked helmet from the Kaiser Wilhelm days, and there was even a curve-bladed cavalry sword.

But this time, such delights were secondary: Mark and Craig came with a purpose.

Mark looked over Morton's shoulder curiously. "What're you working on now?"

"My latest work about hoboes, my boy!" Morton said without a pause in his typing.

"Great! That's what we came to ask you about. We heard you telling Dad about them." In the absence of their father, the boys' workload had lightened considerably, and they decided to put this extra time to good use.

Morton Jewell was flattered when anyone took interest in his work, so he stopped what he was doing and turned to give his full attention to his young guests.

"You do me proud, boys! I've amassed quite a body of research here, as you can see." He gestured to the stacks of books, newspapers, photos, and other miscellaneous documents surrounding him. "I'll do my best to help you out. Ask away!"

"Okay, my first question is, why do the hoboes go to some houses and not to others? We know they don't go to the neighbor's on the other side, but they come to our house all the time," Mark began.

Morton interrupted, "What's that you say? They come to your house all the time? That's not what your Dad told me!"

"You gotta promise not to tell our Dad—he doesn't know, and we don't

173

know what he might do if he finds out. Anyway, Mom never lets them in," Mark continued.

"You got my word on that, m'lad!" Morton promised. "Strange that they keep coming to your house, though, if they're always turned away." He was pensive. "You see, they have a system of signs—codes, if you will—that are meant to identify which are the good houses, and which ones to stay away from."

Craig thought this over. "Um, when you say signs, you mean like messages—for other hoboes?"

"Precisely!"

"Where do they—put them?" Mark inquired.

"One thing I've learned about hoboes: they always carry a knife. So it follows that most of the signs are carved in wood."

Craig jerked suddenly as the light came on. "Would they carve one, like, on our Playhouse?"

Mark shot a quizzical look at Craig.

"You've got it, m'boy! That way, any hobo coming up through the woods would see it."

"Morton, quick! We have something to show you. I think I saw one of those signs on The Playhouse! Maybe you can tell us what it means." Craig was beside himself.

For a big man, Morton was quite agile, particularly when motivated. The three hustled out the Jewell's back door and across the Mosier's backyard to The Playhouse.

"There it is!" Craig announced triumphantly, pointing at the crude etching.

Morton closely inspected the large, deeply incised carving of a plus (+), below which were the rough-hewn letters, "PDP."

"Well, I'll be a monkey's uncle!" Morton exclaimed. "Sure enough, boys! This particular sign means, 'good place for a handout'. Hmmm. Interesting. Are you sure your mother isn't feeding our hobo friends?"

Mark looked at Craig, and the brothers turned their shaking heads to Morton. "We're *positive!*" they said in unison, with shaking voices.

"What's *this* mean?" Mark asked, pointing to the letters, anxious to redirect the conversation.

"Sometimes the hobo leaves his name—or initials—so his buddies will know he was here. That's probably what they are—initials," Morton answered.

"P—D—P," Mark read slowly. "Wonder what it stands for?"

Craig voiced his thoughts. "If we scratch out the sign, will they quit coming?" he asked Morton.

"I have an even better idea. This 'plus' can be altered easily to mean something else. Something that will guarantee no more visits."

"How do we do it? We want them to stop bothering our Mom!" Mark said.

Morton pulled a jackknife from his pocket, and the boys watched as he added two lines to the plus, deftly transforming it into a pound (#) sign. "That ought to do it!" he finished with a flourish.

"*Now* what does it say?" Craig asked.

"'Police officer lives here'!" Morton enunciated meaningfully.

"Holy Moly!" Mark exclaimed. "Maybe now the hoboes will stop bothering Mom!"

"Yeah!" Craig agreed.

"Hmmm." Morton was thinking again. "Think I'll follow up on this. You boys ever been down to the hobo jungle across the Northern Pacific trestle?"

The brothers exchanged startled looks.

"Uh huh—they chased us off!" Craig replied.

"Ah, heck, I've been down there lots of times. I know most of them, and for the most part they're real gentlemen. Treat kids really nice—even protect them from unsavory characters. You have nothing to fear, especially if you're with me. I'll introduce you as my friends. What say you, m'boys?"

"Y'mean, *right now?*" Craig looked to Mark for a way out.

"Okay, let's go!" Mark said.

Craig couldn't believe his ears. But since he always went everywhere with Mark, he sighed uneasily and acquiesced.

10

Morton had graciously declined the boys' invitation to be transported in style aboard The Ship. He had convinced them that his bulk would prove too massive a load for their unseaworthy craft—and there was the very real danger of capsizing and losing his notes. So instead, Morton had driven the few blocks down Water Street and parked by the rose garden. The ever-present capitol dome, topped by its still precariously tilted cupola, loomed close at hand. It was impossible to ignore its presence, and, as usual, it captivated the brothers. Morton usually knew a great deal about such things and enjoyed sharing his knowledge with any and all who would listen. Mark and Craig were perhaps his most avid audience.

"Have you boys been up to the top lately?" he said, making a sweeping gesture toward the dome.

"We tried to once, not too long ago. There was a chain across the elevator door and a big sign that said 'CONDEMNED,'" Mark answered.

"There's another way, besides the elevator," Morton announced. "It's a long climb, but I've been up several times taking pictures for an article I'm writing on Olympia. If you'd like, I'll take you fellows along some time!"

"Neat-o! That'd be great!" Craig gushed.

Mark was skeptical. "You sure it's okay? What happens if we get caught?"

"Never fear. This old seadog has friends in high places. Why, my next door neighbor is the lieutenant governor!"

The brothers shared a laugh, and the three headed for the cement steps that led steeply down the hill to the lake. From there it was a short walk to the trestle and across to the hobo jungle.

Smoke rose from the campfire where a large cast-iron pot simmered perpetually. Morton strode purposefully out ahead of the boys, who were hanging back apprehensively, the haunting memories of their deed rushing back.

"Halloo the camp!" Morton bellowed, his voice rumbling from deep

176

within his chest and reverberating off The Cliffs.

Heads turned throughout the camp, indicating that this kind of visit didn't happen every day. Most faces registered welcome recognition, and choruses of "Hallo Mort!" and "Hey, it's Mort!" echoed around the jungle.

It was at this point that Morton realized the boys had dropped back, and he turned to wave them in.

"Come on, boys! I want to introduce you," he called.

As the boys reluctantly approached, one of the hoboes was heard to say, "Oh, my gawd—it's them boys we chased off! Geez, Mort—if we knowed they was friends with you, we never…"

"Forget it! I brought 'em to introduce you formally and show 'em what fine folks you hoboes are. It seems they got the wrong impression the first time around!"

Freight-train was genuinely contrite as Mort introduced his two young friends, who had joined him but stood uneasily behind him.

Mark and Craig had immediately picked out the hobo who had run them off, and Freight-train, noticing the boys' discomfort, knew what he had to do.

"Mort, you haven't met the newcomer here. SKEDADDLE! Get over here!"

Mark and Craig jumped and were ready to run.

"Hold on there, boys!" Freight-train said with a wide grin, as the hobo called Skedaddle approached sheepishly. "This here fella had just come into our jungle the day you youngsters dropped by. Since he didn't have a road name yet, and since we all got such a hoorah outta him tellin' you boys to skedaddle, that's the handle we gave him!"

The second hobo looked down and shuffled his feet nervously.

"You got somethin' to say to these boys, Skedaddle?" Freight-train admonished.

"Reckon I do. I'm really sorry I skeered you fellers. Didn't s'pect you'd take me serious. Been takin' lotsa guff here from my mates."

"Great Scott!" Morton ejaculated. "Do you lads realize the significance of this event? You just became part of my book—the chapter called 'The Naming of a Hobo'!" He opened his notebook and began scribbling furiously.

Skedaddle smiled warmly at Mark and Craig, who, noticeably relieved, moved forward and took turns shaking his hand. The boys shared a similar thought: *Maybe they aren't all bad!*

Morton looked up from his notes, suddenly recalling the purpose of his mission. Gathering wind, he boomed out to the camp in general.

"Does anyone here use the handle 'PDP'?"

From somewhere outside the circle of the assembled hoboes came a belligerent growl: "PAY DAY PADDY!"

Mark and Craig were transfixed as their gaze fell on the shadowy figure of the now familiar skulking hobo, just as he receded from view.

"Who's there?" Morton asked. There was no response, so Morton turned with a questioning look to Freight-train.

"That's Black Ball. A real bad sort. We don't like him much around here. He doesn't get along with anybody." He looked meaningfully at Mark and Craig. "He *does* like young boys, though," he said in a soft aside to Morton, who was again writing furiously. "Says women are for breeding, and boys are for fun. He sure hasn't earned the right to call himself a hobo!"

"Real sweet guy, eh?" Morton rubbed his chin thoughtfully. "So, tell me about his friend—Pay Day!"

"Interesting you should put it that way," Freight-train came back. "Strangest thing. Everybody likes Pay Day, yet those two're thick as thieves—can't figure it out!"

"Tell me more about Pay Day. How'd he get that handle?" Morton persisted.

"Well, old Pay Day, he keeps to himself pretty much, you know. That is, until Black Ball came along. They fell in together, maybe 'cause they both hit the bottle pretty hard. Seems that every now and then, pretty regular, Pay Day comes into the green. Before Black Ball, he was real generous when he got it. Everybody in the jungle started saying, 'It must be Pay Day!'—so naturally, since we already knew him as Paddy, he took on the handle 'Pay Day Paddy'!"

"What's happened since Black Ball entered the picture?" Morton asked.

"Guess it was all goin' to quench their thirst. 'Course, haven't seen Pay Day in a coon's age, and no one goes near Black Ball. He comes and goes—seen him cross the trestle, so I figure he's lookin' for handouts at those houses over there by the capitol."

Morton slowly, deliberately closed his notebook. He realized the time had come to cut this visit short. Thanking Freight-train profusely, he placed a hand on each of the boys' shoulders, propelling them out of the camp and toward the trestle.

Taking advantage of the sudden turn of events, Craig looked up at Morton excitedly.

"Do we have time to go up into the dome?" he asked.

"Absolutely!" was Morton's emphatic reply.

. . . . .

They climbed the monumental expanse of broad stairs leading to the impressive entrance of the Legislative Building. Craig was especially fascinated as Morton took on the role of consummate tour guide.

Ushering the boys through the portals and into the rotunda with a flourish, he began his monologue. "My boys, you are entering one of the finest capitols in these United States. Its design closely follows that of the capitol in the *other* Washington. When finished in 1928, it had the fourth largest dome—in the world!"

"Wow!" Craig had an early love of such statistical superlatives. "How tall is it?"

"Ahah! You're a man after my own heart," Morton said with satisfaction. "She's precisely 287 feet—or, I should say, she *was*, before our little quake tipped the cupola up there."

"When are they ever going to fix that?" Mark wondered aloud.

"Any year now," Morton chortled. "Actually, I understand it's in the budget for next year." He rambled on informatively about the imported Italian marble, the cost of construction, and the like. He led them across the wide, circular rotunda floor, and both boys craned their necks and gaped up— and up, and up—to the impossibly high, curved alabaster ceiling of the dome within a dome. Two narrow walkways ringed the inside circumference, one about halfway up, and the other at a dizzying height above the rotunda floor. Normally, visitors could be seen leaning over the waist-high railings, marveling at the panorama of the immense open space around and below them—but not since the earthquake and the closing of the elevator.

As they passed the condemned elevator, Morton explained why it was out of service. "When the earthquake hit at its hardest, the elevator car was all the way at the top. The cables were worn and snapped like toothpicks, and down she came. The car smashed flat as a pancake when she hit bottom. It was most fortunate that no one was aboard at the time—but the folks in the cupola had the scare of their lives!"

As Mark and Craig tried to imagine that frightening scene, they followed

Morton around the rotunda to a small, unobtrusive doorway that they had never noticed before.

"This is the only way up now, boys," he announced. "Ready for a climb?"

The boys were amazed at this discovery. After countless trips up the dome, they had always believed there was only one way to reach the cupola atop the dome. And that was first by elevator, which went only as far as the upper walkway; second, up the iron staircase that began at that point and zigzagged its way around the curving inside dome to the base of the cupola; and third, the vertical spiral stairway leading up into the open-air cupola itself.

Craig took off like a shot, jumping up the stairs past Morton. Mark was close on his heels.

"C'mon, Mort!" Craig yelled.

"Go on ahead, lads!" Morton called. "These old legs aren't as young as they used to be! But don't go up into the cupola without me."

Emerging winded and panting from the narrow stairwell at the upper walkway, the brothers knew their way from here. They paused a moment to catch their breath, and then entered the second stairway, made necessary because no elevator could operate around the curvature of the dome.

As many times as they had traversed this section beyond the elevator, it remained eerie and intriguing. The clanging of their feet contacting the metal stairs rang out in the dark emptiness of the space between the inner and outer dome. Bare light bulbs hung at rare intervals, dimly illuminating the stairs and casting ghostlike shadows onto the massive, curved surfaces on both sides of them.

They finally reached the top of the staircase, where it entered a brightly lit enclosure atop the inner dome, at the foot of the spiral staircase. On the side opposite them, there was a door labeled NO ENTRY that had always been locked. The sign had always aroused the boys' curiosity.

"Mark, look! The door's open!"

Mark saw that the door was hanging by one hinge, probably damaged in the earthquake, and now exposing the dark void beyond. They approached the opening slowly and peered through.

It was the other side of the space between the two domes—but narrower. The curvature of the domes made a steep drop, with the outer dome becoming nearly vertical, resulting in a V-shaped space, wide at the top, narrowing abruptly, and joining sharply at the bottom.

Balanced on the sloping edge of the inner dome, just through the doorway inside the space, was a large, wedge-shaped piece of masonry that must have fallen from the ceiling of the outer dome during the earthquake. "No wonder this place was condemned!" Mark exclaimed. "Anybody could fall down in there."

"And never get out!" Craig added in awe.

Just then, a wheezing Morton reached the enclosure, and as Mark turned to greet him, Craig reached through the opening and put his hand on the chunk of masonry.

It moved! It was teetering back and forth, right on the brink.

"Craig—get away from there!" an alarmed Morton huffed. "That side's a deathtrap—what do you think that sign is for!" Completely exhausted, he gestured upward toward the cupola. As the boys began the final climb, he admonished, "And be careful!"

Once they had gained the perch that afforded a bird's-eye view of their hometown, all else was forgotten. Even the cracks in the miniature columns supporting the cupola roof and the new angle of inclination could not detract from the euphoria of their wondrous height.

And now the brothers, alone among all their friends, knew the secret way to the top.

PART VI

A bright crimson line on the eastern Pacific horizon marked the first light of predawn, but the Kalihiwai estate was still shrouded in the darkness of night. The Mosier brothers remained suspended in time, spellbound by their journey into the past.

"Yeah, ol' Mort must have had the whole thing figured out," Mark contemplated. "Wonder if Dad ever did."

"I guess we'll never know now," Craig said, groping blindly in the box for the next item. He withdrew an old, faded snapshot, only dimly visible in the dwindling flames from the tiki torches. He held it close for a better look, and as he did so, Mark noticed that after half a century, Craig's glasses still had that penchant to slip down on his nose at the most inopportune moments.

"Oh, my God...." Craig's words came slowly, as he squinted to see. He handed the photo to Mark without a word.

"Isn't that Tito?" Mark breathed.

"...With Tippi!" Craig added emphatically. "Remember how much she loved Tito?"

Mark was lost in thought. As he turned to speak, Craig could swear he saw Mark's eyes flashing green, even in the dim light of the torches. Mark lost control, leaping to his feet and kicking his deck chair onto its side. He paced furiously to and fro on the lanai. Suddenly he gripped the railing tightly with both hands, leaned far out, and bellowed at the top of his lungs.

"That Goddamn miserable son-of-a-bitch! I'd kill him again if I had the chance!"

Craig heard Mark's roar echoing up Kalihiwai Valley and fading into the distance. Craig had been at Mark's side on such occasions before, and he was perhaps the only person who understood his brother's pain. He went to Mark's side and placed his arm around his wide shoulders. Long pent-up sobs wracked Mark's body as he turned to embrace his younger brother.

"It's okay, Mark—it's all behind us now...." Craig's voice choked off.

They stood together at the railing for a long time, neither one able to speak.

1

The Mosier bayplace was located on Eld Inlet, about a fifteen-mile drive west of the house on Water Street. It was a rickety, battered old cabin that had been built in an ill-conceived position partially over a swamp. Ray and C.I. had improved it considerably over the years. Mark and Craig could remember that, not long before, there had been an outhouse a hundred feet or so to the rear, reached on rotten planks haphazardly placed across the swamp. As they would approach the outhouse on the squishy boards, the pungent odor of skunk cabbage would give in to a more overpowering stench. They would take care to keep their balance on the walkway to avoid stinging nettles that lined both sides. Then they would waste no time completing their business, or suffer the consequences of many mosquito bites in tender areas.

But now, there was a bathroom *inside* the cabin. As if this weren't luxury enough, newfangled electricity had replaced the old kerosene lamps and Coleman stove. Not only that, they even had an ancient monitor-top Frigidaire; no more need for the big block of ice that once cooled the old ice box and had to be brought with them on every trip to the cabin.

Before improvements, C.I. and Hattie's cabin had been a one-room shack. Now, besides the bathroom, there was a large, separate bedroom in the back. Most of the family's time, though, was spent on the big, veranda-like porch that faced out toward the bay.

This was their first trip down the bay since before their father's operation last fall. Spring vacation, 1953, had arrived, and Mark and Craig had prevailed upon their parents to observe the family's traditional first visit of the season to the bayplace.

The boys made an effort to escape as they arrived at the cabin, but their father had other ideas.

"Hey, you kids! You unload the car before you take off!"

Their father still yelled at them, but it was different now. Since the operation, Ray had not laid a hand on them. The tyrannical outbursts that had led to his violent attacks had ceased altogether. Their mother had explained

187

the old war injury that had caused his erratic behavior, and that she was sure things would be better now. She had been right so far, and the quality of the boys' lives had improved immeasurably.

Years of abuse, though, had conditioned the brothers to respond with fear whenever addressed by their father. So without hesitation, they obediently began carrying the week's supplies into the cabin.

"Anything else, Mom?" Mark asked as they completed their task.

"That'll do it. Be back in time for dinner!" Vicky said cheerfully.

"Thanks, boys!" Ray called after them, to their shocked surprise. Outside the cabin, Craig said incredulously, "Wow, has Dad ever changed—did he really *thank* us?"

"Yeah—wonder how long this will last," retorted Mark, the incurable skeptic.

With that, they made good their escape. "C'mon, Tito!" Craig hollered as they picked up speed.

"Let's go exploring!" Mark suggested.

"Where?

"Across the road. I want to see that pond Karl told us about."

Craig didn't remember hearing about any pond. But he was always willing to follow Mark's lead.

They started up the steep, winding wagon track that was the only access from the main road to the cabin. The steepest part was always wet and slippery from springwater seeping across. Before attempting to leave the cabin by car, it was common to hear, "Let's take a run at it," since it was necessary to gain sufficient speed to make the grade and avoid getting stuck in the mud.

Off to the right was a ravine the brothers had named Red River Valley after the little stream that flowed through it, which left a reddish residue on the gravel. Years of fallen leaves had eliminated the undergrowth and had produced a parklike appearance, coloring the ground in shades of red and brown.

They reached the top of the driveway where it met the road. Instinctively, they took hold of Tito's collar until they could determine if it was safe to cross. This was tricky because visibility was poor on the narrow road, which curved sharply where it approached from their left, dipped down to where they were, then rose abruptly into an impossibly steep hill to their right. Invariably, cars would round the bend without warning, drivers gunning their engines to make that hill. So, it was the boys' practice to look and listen before they crossed the road, which was not often, and then to run across with Tito in hand.

The woods across the road were dark and thick with underbrush, in stark contrast to Red River Valley. Suddenly freed, Tito vanished into the brush, noisily marking his progress. It was much slower going for Mark and Craig, and they began to wonder if Karl had given them a bum steer.

After awhile, Craig said, "Let's go back."

"Yeah, okay," Mark agreed. Then, "Wait a sec—what's that over there?"

"Hey, neat! It's a clearing!"

"It looks like a little meadow," Mark added. They marveled silently at the luxuriant green that had the appearance of freshly mown grass.

Tito must have spotted it too, for as they spoke he shot out of the underbrush and onto its inviting surface. His flying feet touched down—and down—and down—as his entire body followed and sank from sight, a black geyser of water shooting skyward. The meadow had opened up and swallowed their dog!

As they watched, concentric circles of black water spread out, and their green meadow was gone. At this very moment Tito surfaced, spluttering and choking, his front legs pawing for the sky, his bewildered expression seeming to say, "Why am I swimming?" As he clambered ashore, the boys watched in amazement as the disturbed surface calmed and almost magically became green again.

"Poor Tito!" Mark said in mock pity. "C'mere, boy!"

Head held low, the bedraggled dog crept sheepishly over to his young masters for some much-needed solace. Instinct took hold, however, and he shook himself for all he was worth, instantly spraying the boys from head to foot, then standing and looking pleased with himself.

"Tito!" Mark yelped, all thought of solace forgotten.

Looking back once more at the smooth, emerald surface, Craig had an inspiration.

"Let's call it Green Lake!"

And so it was.

2

The bright morning sunlight filled the little cabin with warm cheer. Mark and Craig had risen with the sun, knowing that there was to be an early low tide, ideal for clam digging. One of their standing orders was to dig a load of the savory rock clams from the mud flats exposed in front of the cabin at the first low tide of each visit. This was one chore the brothers did not mind, and Tito loved it. He would run ahead down the beach, picking a spot and pawing at the mud, turning with a quizzical look at the boys, as if to say, "How about here?" Somehow, he always knew where the clams were in greatest abundance, so the boys followed his lead.

As Tito waited impatiently, Mark and Craig paused for a moment, not wanting to disturb the perfect stillness of the early morning scene. The mirrored surface of the bay was motionless, reflecting the forested shoreline on the other side of the inlet. Today was a rare, crystal clear day, and the great snowcapped peak of Mount Rainier seemed closer than ever, glimmering behind the leaning fir tree, a victim of some long-ago storm that pointed to the mountain, revealing its location in fair weather or foul.

From far across the bay came the faint echoes of someone chopping wood, followed by a barking dog. The moment was gone, the silence of this morning forever broken, and the brothers and their dog bent to their task.

Turning over the mud with their short-handled spades, they began filling the bucket with fat, juicy specimens. Craig finally had a chance to say what was on his mind and, leaning on his shovel, he turned to Mark.

"Where did you say you hid the hobo's hat after Timmy found it?"

"Why?" Mark asked, jolted by this sudden—and unwelcome—question.

"'Cuz I don't think it's there anymore, that's why!" Craig answered.

"Of course it's there, stupid! Who would ever take it? You probably just forgot where I put it!"

"You told me you put it in the big bin outside The Playhouse!"

This startled Mark, and he stood up and faced his little brother.

"That's where I put it, okay. But I hid it in the corner under a bunch of wood. Did you look there?"

"I looked everywhere in there, and I didn't see it."

"What were you looking for? You shouldn't even be opening that bin!" Mark was really annoyed, and Craig looked down at his feet and kept quiet. After awhile, Mark spoke again.

"I'm sure you just didn't look good enough—you gotta clean your glasses more often! I'll find it when we get home."

. . . . .

By the end of that day Mark knew he couldn't wait a whole week to find out about the hat. Since Ray was commuting each day to work in Olympia, Mark fabricated a reason for the boys to ride in with him on Monday morning. They took Tito along, since they anticipated a day in the woods, enjoying the rope swing, possibly a dip at The Point with Tippi.

Ray dropped the threesome off at the big house on Water Street just before eight o'clock that morning, and Mark went straight for the bin. He banged open the hinged lid and zeroed in on the spot where he had hidden the hat almost a year ago. Panicking, he frantically thrust aside the bits of scrap lumber and other debris.

"It's gotta be here somewhere!" he gasped, not finding it.

"I told ya!" Craig said, feeling smug at being right, but sobered by the gravity of the dilemma. He put one hand against The Playhouse for support, and stiffened as something caught his eye.

"C'mon, Craig—what are you doing? We gotta—" Mark was cut off by Craig's exclamation.

"Mark! Look at this!"

Mark joined his brother, who was pointing a shaky finger in front of him.

There on The Playhouse wall was the hobo sign, now crudely defaced.

A deep, jagged 'X' had been gouged through the initials PDP, in effect crossing them out. Above the X, rough new initials had been hewn.

"'BB'!" the boys mouthed in unison. The silence was palpable.

Finally, hesitatingly, Craig stuttered, "B-B—Black Ball!"

"Who's that? Oh, yeah—the guy at the hobo jungle—the one nobody liked!"

"The one I saw walkin' around here that time," Craig said tremulously.

"You—you don't think—" Mark's words faltered.

"The hat—*he must have the hat!*" Craig finished.

"If he does, he must know we killed Pay Day Paddy—and we're in for it!"

"Wh—what should we do?"

"Let's get Morton. Maybe he can help us," Mark said.

Craig thought this over. "You don't think we should tell him the whole story, do you?"

"'Course not! I just want to find out if he knows anything about this guy Black Ball—and if he's seen him coming around."

Knowing Morton was not an early riser, the brothers went cautiously down the hill to The Room, with Tito charging ahead as usual. They often used this tree-lined enclosure for discussions of a serious nature.

Just as they approached the narrow opening, they scared up some wild animal, and Tito took off after it in hot pursuit, his frenzied yipping fading into the distance.

"Probably one of those silver foxes he always chases and never catches," Craig commented.

"Yeah, he'll be back when he gets tired. We need to decide what we're gonna say to Mort," Mark added, sliding between two tree trunks into The Room.

. . . . .

Morton, standing next to Mark and Craig at the Playhouse, was visibly shaken by the change to the hobo sign. He remembered with deep concern what Freight-train had told him about Black Ball's penchant for young boys.

"I have some good news for you young gents," Morton began. "I was down at the jungle just two days ago, trying to learn more about this fellow Black Ball. They told me they'd had enough of him, that he was no longer welcome in their camp. Apparently he had lived up to his name. Freight-train told me he'd been 'blackballed' from camps coast to coast before he landed here. They made sure he was on the next freight out of town. That was two weeks back, and no one's seen him since."

Mark and Craig showed obvious relief. Morton, taking note, thought a word of caution was in order.

"But if you should ever see him again, make yourselves scarce. He's not to be trifled with—you don't want to meet *this* guy in a dark alley!"

The rest of the day was spent in the woods, mostly whiling away the hours on the rope swing. Late that afternoon, Craig remembered they hadn't seen Tito since he took off on his chase early that morning.

"Hey, Mark, we better go find Tito before Dad gets here!"

Mark agreed, and they headed deeper into the woods, taking turns calling out their pet's name.

Calls of "Tiii-to! Tiii-to!" resounded eerily far into the depths of their forested playground and floated back to them plaintively on misty breezes.

But there was no response from their beloved companion.

Tito had been known to run off for several days at a time, so the boys did not think this was a matter of great concern—except for the fact that they were spending the week down the bay and wouldn't be home when he came back.

The boys were still deep in the woods when the faint sound of their father's prearranged tooting signal reached their ears. They called off their search and headed back up the hill.

Reaching the top, Craig told Mark to go on ahead, and said, "Tell Dad I'll be right there. I'll put some food out for Tito."

On the drive back to the bayplace, Ray agreed to stop by the house every day to check for Tito.

3

The next few days dragged by. Each evening, the boys rushed anxiously to greet their father as the car came rolling down the wagon track and pulled to a stop beside the cabin. And each evening came the same disappointing report: no sign of Tito.

By Friday, the brothers were so worried that they decided to ride in with Ray again and spend the day searching for their missing pet. They planned to enlist the help of Tippi, who knew the woods as well as themselves. She accepted enthusiastically.

"I saw him just the other day—I think Wednesday," Tippi reassured them. "He came up to me for some loving, and he looked fine. If I'd known you guys weren't around, I would've looked after him."

"Hey, that's great! At least we know he's okay. We should be able to find him today." Then Mark explained the plan.

They each started from a different part of Water Street, Tippi on the left flank, Mark on the right, and Craig in the middle. They worked their way slowly down through the woods and eventually converged at The Point. It went according to plan, except that they failed to find Tito. Hot and tired, the three collapsed on the grassy knoll overlooking their favorite swimming hole.

Tippi rolled over seductively onto her back, showing off her tender young breasts, erect nipples thrusting tautly against the sheer cotton of her white summer dress. She was flirtatiously swishing the skirt to and fro, slowly raising it to tantalize the boys.

"Mmmmmm! The sun feels so good!" she murmured, as the frilly hemline rose above her tanned knees. Boldly, in a sudden unexpected move, she leaped to her feet and lifted the dress over her head, exposing her lovely nakedness to the two shocked brothers.

"Last one in's a rotten egg!" she tossed musically back over her shoulder as she ran for the water. As she performed one of her perfect dives, the boys watched her legs part slightly, invitingly.

Mark recovered enough to rasp hoarsely, "Sh-sh-she's not wearing any panties!"

"Let's go!" Craig had no second thoughts, as he awkwardly pulled off his clothes and ran to join Tippi.

Mark was taken aback by his brother's quick action and sat there, dazed.

Tippi showed her pleasure at Craig's response by swimming over next to him. She chided his older brother. "Whatsa matter Mark—Craig's not afraid!"

Mark had to do something, so he turned his back and slowly began to undress.

"Come on, Mark—you got something to hide?" Tippi taunted.

While waiting for Mark to join them, Tippi submerged one hand, delicately touching Craig, and then slipping her warm fingers around his exposed penis. Craig squealed, delighting in this new experience.

Mark, not quite sure what was going on but not wanting to miss out on anything, almost tripped over his pants in his sudden rush to join them. Tippi greeted him with a wide grin and placed her other hand around his growing manhood.

"Oooooo! What's happening down there, Mark?" Tippi said provocatively. Mark, for the first time in his life, was speechless.

Tugging gently on them, pulling them toward the bank, she had them totally under her spell.

"Come with me, you guys—I have an idea! But it has to be in The Playhouse," she purred, suggestively emphasizing her point by giving them each a final squeeze.

Tippi was now the only thing on their minds. Everything in their lives was temporarily forgotten—even Tito. They were consumed by fantasies of what awaited them in The Playhouse.

Mark and Craig did their best to keep up with Tippi on their way to The Playhouse. Their clothes clung uncomfortably to their wet bodies, and certain parts of their anatomies, especially Mark's, were getting in the way. But there was no doubt about what lay ahead—Tippi made sure of that, swaying her hips temptingly when she knew the boys were watching.

Once, gaining the top of a promontory affording an especially fine view to the brothers below her, she sexily raised her skirt to her thighs and did a little dance for their benefit.

Again, at the top of the hill, she stopped long enough for them to catch up, and her intimate caresses renewed the promise of things to come. Giggling, she ran gracefully ahead to The Playhouse door, and pulled it open.

Tippi's piercing shriek filled the air and left the boys' ears ringing. She streaked past them, still screaming, and disappeared from sight.

Mark and Craig moved in stunned silence toward the open Playhouse door, terrified at what they might find. Mark saw it first.

"Noooo! Oh, God, no—!"

Sitting in a pool of blood on The Playhouse floor was the severed head of their lost dog Tito. His lifeless eyes penetrated their very souls. Perched diabolically on the head was…the hobo's hat! A note was pinned to it. Eyes stinging with tears, shaking violently, Mark sobbed uncontrollably as he read the scrawled words:

YER NEXT

BB

Craig had gone catatonic and collapsed to the floor. His pupils rolled upward into his head and he was about to pass out.

Mark acted on instinct alone. Death permeated the air around them. The thought of escape possessed him.

He shook Craig out of his stupor, pulled him to his feet, and yanked him out the door.

"Craig—Craig! Snap out of it! We gotta get out of here!"

Wild-eyed, they charged out to Water Street. Mark, sensing movement behind him, looked around. He saw a figure stumbling around the corner of the garage.

It was Black Ball, lunging mindlessly toward them.

"Craig! Run for your life!" Mark yelled. Without thinking logically, Mark started sprinting down Water Street, Craig by his side.

"Where we goin'?"

"Just keep up with me! Maybe he won't follow us."

Glancing over their shoulders, they saw Mark was wrong.

Both boys were thinking the same thought: that they might lose the hobo by leading him into the maze of tunnels and walkways that connected the capitol buildings underground. They put all the stamina of their young bodies into gaining the sanctuary of the first building ahead of their pursuer, who, after all, was not in the best physical condition. They succeeded in pulling ahead, and, entering the Lands Building, they were relieved to see that he was some distance behind—but not far enough to lose sight of them and follow them into the tunnel to the domed Legislative Building.

As they picked up speed in the long, straight section of the tunnel, an idea struck Craig like a bombshell.

"Mark!" he wheezed. "The stairs—up the dome!"

Mark remembered the secret way to the top Morton had shown them. This just might be the answer!

"Okay!" Mark puffed, more out of breath than his little brother. "Y-you lead—you know the way better!"

Craig knew the labyrinth of passageways and how they accessed the various buildings from his old newspaper route. He made a quick turn up a flight of stairs, and the brothers emerged into the cavernous, marble-encased rotunda at the base of the capitol dome.

"Hurry!" Craig panted, running across the polished floor. His feet slipped away and he fell, sliding harmlessly into the wall on the far side. The moment's delay was costly. Just as Mark pulled Craig into the narrow landing, Black Ball emerged from the other side and spotted him.

Where *was* everybody? There was no one to witness the hell-bent madman careening after his quarry.

"Damn! He saw us!" Mark whispered in dismay, realizing their secret had been compromised. "Now we're trapped!"

"Climb like crazy!" Craig shouted, his voice ringing up the unseen reaches of the stairwell. "I have an idea!" They began leaping up two and three steps at a time.

They thought they had a good lead when a roar came out of the gloom, surrounding them with its power and shaking them to the core.

"Hah! Now I've got ya! I'll cut yer guts out!" The thunderous yell echoed around them.

Was he upon them?

Paused in utter silence, they heard his feet on the steps—he was still a good distance below!

Reaching the upper circular walkway, close to exhaustion, the boys stopped again to listen. They heard their pursuer far below, his labored breathing and his intermittent footfalls revealing his slow but persistent progress up the stairs. During this brief moment of recovery, Mark managed to choke out a few words.

"S-so—what's…your idea? Push…him down…the elevator shaft?"

"No—better'n that!" Craig said, already nearly back to normal. Resuming the climb, he clanged up the metal staircase that led around the open space between the two domes.

Mark doggedly followed him into the blackness. Craig's newfound determination reduced Mark to the unaccustomed role of follower. He knew Craig's idea was all they had.

Entering the enclosure at the base of the spiral staircase well ahead of Black Ball, Mark and Craig slumped limply to the floor. As soon as he could speak coherently, Craig fired out his plan. Mark nodded his approval, greatly relieved. He knew it could work and felt pride surging within him for his little brother.

Mark also felt the strength coming back into his tired limbs, along with that invincible feeling only young boys know.

The two boys took up their positions. Craig got down on his hands and knees in front of the no-entry doorway and feigned exhaustion. Mark climbed up the spiral staircase just far enough to be out of sight—and not a moment too soon.

The door on the other side burst open and in stumbled the hobo, berserk with rage. His face was a mask of hatred, veins bulging on his neck, sweat pouring off his brow. Raised menacingly in his right hand was a giant, jagged hunting knife. He spied Craig cringing on the floor.

The guttural snarls that came from his slobbering lips were almost unintelligible.

"Ahm…gonna…cut yer prick off…and make you watch me…eat it!"

Black Ball staggered off-balance toward defenseless Craig, who was now whimpering piteously.

As the hobo passed the spiral stairway, Mark jumped down and ran furiously toward him, vengeance glowing hotly from his green eyes. He made contact, pushing the startled man with all his might from behind. At the same instant, Craig scrambled out of the way. The timing was perfect. Mark's push combined with Black Ball's forward momentum sent the hapless hobo flying through the doorway and into the space beyond. Blackness engulfed him.

He seemed to be airborne for a long moment before the boys heard the *WHUMP!* of his heavy landing at the bottom of the V where the domes met. This was soon followed by groans, then yells, and the scritching sound of his fingernails against the inner dome as he tried futilely to climb out of the dark chasm. His shrieked threats of dismemberment and murder curdled their blood.

"C'mon Mark, like I told you—it's really loose!"

As one, the brothers leaned forward and placed their hands firmly on the wedge-shaped chunk of masonry. It gave way so suddenly, the boys almost went with it, and Mark had to grab Craig's belt to prevent him from falling too.

The heavy concrete slab, its sharp leading edge pointing downward, began its noisy descent.

"THIS IS FOR TITO, YOU ROTTEN SON-OF-A-BITCH!" Mark howled into the void.

A scream like a banshee rose from the depths, cut off in the instant that the plummeting slab wedged itself tightly into the V formerly occupied by Black Ball.

4

The silence of a tomb enveloped them. They collapsed into a trance, and time was meaningless. It wasn't until Craig began to laugh that Mark stirred.

It began quietly, but grew louder. The cackle seemed to feed on itself. It reverberated eerily between the domes. Hearing it, Mark thought that Craig had gone mad.

"Craig!" he yelled, pulling on his arm.

Mark could see the whites of Craig's eyes, opened wide, dilated pupils darting back and forth. He was gasping for breath. It suddenly occurred to Mark that the air was heavy and close in the small enclosure. They needed fresh air.

Craig was now laughing hysterically. Mark pulled him to his feet and began dragging him up the spiral stairs toward the cupola.

"Black Ball—had a fall—!" Craig wheezed between gasps.

"Craig, shut up! Save your breath!" But Craig continued, giggles punctuating his diabolical rhyme:

"Black Ball had a fall
"He got stuck in the capitol wall
"He couldn't climb and he couldn't crawl
"So we wedged him in—*for good and all!*"

When he was finished, Craig dissolved in a fit of short choking sounds that came partly from his nose and partly from his throat. It couldn't really be called laughing. Mark thought it was the most hideous sound he'd ever heard, and it was all around him. He doggedly struggled upward, pulling on the handrail, fearing for Craig's sanity.

They reached the top, entering the little circular enclosure leading to the open-air cupola. Mark opened the metal door. Sunlight streamed in and cool breezes flowed over them. The effect was like a tonic to Craig.

The cupola was encircled by a four-foot high concrete barrier. Mark led the way down the tilted floor and they leaned against the barrier, swallowing the wonderful air in great gulps. Craig had stopped laughing and fallen silent. Mark kept a concerned eye on him but said nothing for a long time.

How much time passed they could not tell. Finally, Mark said, "No one will ever find him there, I bet!" It was mostly to reassure himself. He wasn't expecting Craig to answer.

"Do you think—anybody saw him chasing us up here?" Apparently, Craig was back to his senses!

Mark paused, deciding not to mention Craig's frightening lapse. "I think they'd be here by now if they did."

"We have to go back down, past—" Craig cut off. Numbly, he remembered the deed.

"—hobo number two!" Mark finished. "At least we don't have to bury this one!" He jerked suddenly, looking at Craig.

Craig looked back aghast.

"TITO!" they exclaimed in unison.

They still had unfinished business—in The Playhouse—and very little time.

. . . . .

Mark and Craig slowed as they approached the garage on Water Street. A growing feeling of dread crept over them.

"How...can we...?" Craig began hesitatingly.

Mark glanced around the garage. "There's a gunnysack over there. Let's put—it—in there and bury it!"

"Wh—where?" Craig wanted to know.

"How about where we buried the hobo?"

Craig wasn't too happy with this. "How we gonna get Tito—I mean—his head—the head—how we gonna get it in the gunnysack?" Craig couldn't bear the thought of touching—or even seeing—the hideous thing Black Ball's evil heart—and jagged knife—had wrought.

Mark's plan took shape as he spotted the long-handled shovel.

"If you help me bury it, I'll—get it into the sack," Mark said waveringly.

Craig was peering toward The Playhouse through the dusty garage window. "Omigosh! The door's wide open!"

"Let's get this over with. All we can hope is that nobody saw it!"

The Playhouse loomed like an apparition as the boys approached. Craig hung off to the side by the storage bin.

Mark's stomach convulsed as he reached The Playhouse door. He swallowed hard, trying to control the nausea threatening to overwhelm him. Keeping his eyes averted as much as possible from the awful scene, he held his breath. Holding the gunnysack open with his left hand and gripping the shovel firmly in his right, in one swift movement he scooped the head—and the hat—into the bag and out of sight.

With great relief, Mark's eyes came to focus on the floor where the head had rested.

There in a pool of coagulating blood was a gray, gelatinous mass that had drained from Tito's severed head. Mark's stomach turned inside out, and bile rose in his throat as he vomited uncontrollably.

Craig forced himself to look in, and not seeing the head, came to his stricken brother's side. "Mark! Wh—!" At that moment, Craig saw the cause of Mark's retching and bolted out the door, suddenly very sick himself.

After nothing was left to throw up, they continued heaving, unable to talk. But grimly they set to work, driven by something inside them they could not understand. In a daze, not letting their conscious minds deal with the physical task, they neared the completion of the cleanup. Still oblivious, Mark cast around for a rag to finish the job. His eyes fell on what appeared to be a knapsack. Craig heard Mark's sudden gasp.

"Huh?"

"Lookit this—!" Mark jerked his head around The Playhouse. "And over there—it's a shirt!"

"And—on that bench—it—it's a sleeping bag!"

"My God...he was—living here!" Mark was incredulous.

"And everyone thought he'd left for good," Craig added.

Mark considered. "Yeah. So we gotta bury all this stuff, too!"

"And then nobody will ever know," Craig finished.

5

Having stuffed Black Ball's worldly possessions into the gunnysack—taking care not to look within—Mark glanced around The Playhouse. Satisfied that all was in order, he turned to Craig.

"You carry the shovel—I'll take this!" He gingerly lifted the gunny sack, holding it away from his body to avoid any contact, and headed out the door. "Close the door!"

"We—we prob'ly should lock this," Craig offered.

"Good idea—I know where there's an extra padlock in the garage. But we gotta do this first!"

As he went over the crest of the hill, Mark was feeling enough better to make a light-hearted comment. "At least it's daylight this time!"

"Thank goodness—is there any more good news?" Craig answered sarcastically.

Down in the woods, below the old rope swing, the brothers swung left and hesitantly approached the gravesite. They had given this spot a wide berth ever since that fateful, frightening night.

"Wow—you'd never know—something was buried here," Mark said.

"H-how deep—this time?" Craig asked fearfully.

"Just deep enough!" Mark answered, thrusting the shovel into the ground with grim determination. He wanted this nightmare to finally come to an end. He set to work feverishly, dumping shovelfuls of dirt at Craig's feet.

"Watch it, Mark! You're getting it all over my shoes!" No sooner were the words out of Craig's mouth than something flew off Mark's shovel and hit him on the shin. "Ow! What's that?" Craig stooped down to pick up a metallic object, flicking away small clods of dirt clinging to its surface. Mark paused in his digging to see what Craig was holding.

"Hey! That looks like Dad's Medal of Honor!" Mark exclaimed.

"What's it doing down here—in the grave?" Mark snatched it excitedly from Craig's grasp.

"Lemme see it!" He was turning it over in his hands. "C-Craig! Look! R-read this! Oh my God!"

Craig squinted at the small engraved letters and read aloud:

"John 'Ab' Normal"

Mark had slumped to the ground and was sitting in the loose dirt, a blank stare on his face. *This isn't possible,* he thought. Craig was watching his brother in bewilderment.

"D-did we kill—?" Craig stammered.

Mark was still deep in thought. There was no other explanation: the hobo signs on The Playhouse, The War Story, Pay Day Paddy's regular income—and now Ab's Medal of Honor—in the hobo's grave!

"Craig…Pay Day Paddy was…Ab-Normal!"

"You mean—Dad's best friend in the war—was P-Pay Day Paddy? And he was the guy who tried to get Mom?" Craig thought out loud. It all fell into place. "Y-you mean, we killed Ab-Normal?"

"That's right. *We killed Ab-Normal!*" Mark repeated emphatically. "And now we're gonna bury his medal right here with him." Mark got up to resume digging. "Let's get busy and get this over with—Dad will be here pretty soon!"

"Wait a second, Mark! If we killed Ab-Normal, we should be heroes! He was the spy who got all those ships sunk in the war. Now we can tell!"

Mark looked at Craig as if his little brother had lost his mind after all. "Are you crazy? We can't tell!"

"Why not?" Craig demanded.

Mark was angry at having to explain. He flung a couple of shovels of dirt in Craig's direction.

"Boy, Craig, sometimes you're really stupid. While we're at it, why don't we tell them about Black Ball—and of course, what happened to Tito—no one would *ever* believe a story like that!" Mark exploded.

"Well, Black Ball was gonna kill us! I don't see why we can't tell now. Why do we hafta keep it secret?" Craig was adamant.

"Don't forget—Dad doesn't even know Mom was *feeding* the hoboes!"

"Yeah, but Dad's a lot better now," Craig reminded his brother.

"Craig, *think*, blast it! What do you think Dad might do if he found out Mom was attacked?" The shrillness in Mark's voice betrayed his growing exasperation.

"Probably thank us for killing the guy that did it!" Craig insisted.

That was it for Mark. Throwing the shovel aside in disgust, he pounced on little Craig and pushed him to the ground. Craig's glasses flew into the bushes.

"Hey! Cut it out!"

Mark sat atop Craig menacingly and punctuated each word with a vicious stab of his forefinger at his brother's face.

"DAMMIT—YOU—STUPID—IDIOT—LISTEN! We promised Mom we wouldn't tell! We promised *MOM!*"

Mark's eyes blazed with a green so intense that, even without his glasses, Craig saw. Mark's argument struck home.

"Okay! Okay! Let me up! Where's my glasses?"

Mark's fury abated, but he stayed where he was, glaring down at Craig.

"So, you're never going to tell—*right?*"

"Right. I—forgot about Mom," Craig said in meek surrender.

Mark removed his bulk and retrieved Craig's glasses from the bushes. Craig regained his feet, brushing the loose dirt from his clothing. Resignedly, he bent to pick up the medal Mark had dropped. He threw it into the grave in disgust.

"There! Hope that makes you happy."

Mark frowned and shook his head, but said nothing. His shovel had the last say.

. . . . .

The grisly business over, Mark and Craig sat on the front porch steps waiting for their father to come for them.

"Do we have time to go see Tippi?" Craig pondered.

"Not today."

"What're we gonna tell Mom and Dad about Tito?" Craig persisted.

"How about, we found him dead in the street, run over by a car. So we put him in a box and buried him down in the woods."

"But what if Tippi tells what really happened?" Craig wouldn't leave it alone.

"Hey, Craig! I don't have all the answers. We better just hope Tippi doesn't tell. But if she does, we can always say she made it up. She always did tell strange stories."

It was the best Mark could do under the circumstances. Now that the brothers finally had a few idle moments, the devastating events of the day were catching up with them. Grief and exhaustion left them numb, shielding them from the emotional trauma that was sure to follow.

Craig had a fleeting image of some future time, of men digging, uncovering it all, trying to piece it together.

They fell silent in their weariness, expressionless eyes staring absently, seeing nothing.

PART VII

The brothers were still standing at the railing when Craig finally broke the long silence. "Next time we're on the mainland, we should go see Tippi again."

"I wonder if there's been any change—the way she just sits there and stares into space—it's so depressing to see her like that." Mark wiped away the last of his tears.

"They say she's never uttered a word since that day at The Playhouse," Craig added sadly.

"Just stares into space…".

"Poor Tippi—but at least our secret is safe with her."

"Amen!" Mark whispered.

The two men shuffled slowly back, and Mark righted his deck chair. Craig settled into his own chair and, pulling back the flaps of the cardboard box, peered within.

"What's left?" Mark asked.

"Not much. There's a few things here, and—what's this? Well, I'll be damned! It's a strongbox—it's got a lock on it!"

"Let's save it 'til last." Mark reached in and removed a framed document. "Listen to this: 'Raymond B. Mosier is hereby designated Governor of the Sovereign State of Washington, having been duly elected by the people to fulfill the duties of Chief Executive during the period January 20, 1956 to January 20, 1960.'" Handing it to Craig, he added, "There's the official state seal!"

"His first term," Craig remarked. "Remember what that meant?"

Mark smiled nostalgically. "The end of life as we knew it—but the end of our nightmare, too."

"We were really worried somebody might find that grave after we moved into the governor's mansion. Remember how we used to walk up to the old house every so often and check it out?"

"Like it was yesterday," Mark replied.

1

For eleven years, Water Street had been their entire world. They still thought of the big old house as home, even though their parents now had it up for sale. Home was now the stately brick mansion that came with the office of governor.

The Mosier brothers were mature beyond their years. Four years ago today their nightmare had begun with the killing of Pay Day Paddy. They had kept this secret, and the terrible events which followed, to themselves. The bond that had existed almost from birth had been strengthened beyond measure by the passage of time and the memories that they alone shared.

They had already faced the fear of being discovered when the cupola, damaged in the earthquake of '49, was finally replaced a year ago. It wasn't until the job was complete, and no unusual reports had been forthcoming, that they knew their fears were unfounded. Black Ball now existed only in the brothers' minds.

The sun shone brightly on this fine spring day. Mark and Craig walked shoulder to shoulder up the familiar street, in what had become a weekly routine. The Japanese flowering cherry trees were in full bloom, and the panoply of pink blossoms floated about their feet.

Faintly in the distance came the screeching and rattling of some sort of machine, interrupted occasionally by the roaring acceleration of a mighty engine. The intensity of the sound increased with every step.

Of one mind as always, the two exchanged glances and wordlessly quickened their step.

"You don't think—" Craig began.

"—it's coming from—" Mark continued.

"—*OUR HOUSE!*" Craig finished.

Now they broke into a dead run. Craig had grown tall, and the two boys were now equally fast.

At Eighteenth they slowed to a halt, the scene now open to them. A huge yellow monster was wreaking havoc where once they lived, ate, slept, and played.

Speechless, they watched as the gigantic, ruthless blade of the bulldozer smashed into the last wall left standing, rending timbers asunder, loosing ancient dust, and sending a hail of splinters skyward. The sound of the crash sent a chill through their hearts, and gooseflesh rose until it ached. In that moment, they saw their childhood passing away with a cruel finality. The house was gone—and so, too, was the beloved maple tree they had climbed so many times. Even the rhododendrons, the holly trees—where was that other roar coming from?

Not the woods! Surely, they wouldn't—!

They ran through the rubble of their fallen house over to where The Playhouse lay in ruins. Tears glistened in Mark's eyes and Craig was crying openly.

The woods were no more. The rope swing, The Throne, The Room—all gone. The bastards! Mark and Craig stood gazing at the wide swath they had cut through the trees, all the way down to the lake. It would never be the same again.

But wait! Over to the left, a monstrous heap of earth was being pushed down the hill. Load upon load had already been dumped until there was now a mountain of dirt above the level where they used to play. And the mountain was right on top of...the hobo's grave!

The brothers lingered on until late in the afternoon, letting it all sink in. The significance of that day was not lost on them.

. . . . .

That night Craig drifted into a fitful sleep, with visions of the rubble that had been their former home vivid in his mind. The full moon cast its light through the window of his bedroom on the third floor of the mansion. In that indefinable space between waking and sleeping, Craig thought he felt Mark tugging on his arm and whispering urgently.

"Come on, Craig! We've got to go back to The Playhouse!"

Not really knowing why, Craig obeyed and got out of bed. As if watching from afar, he was aware of following his brother up Water Street. Mark strode deliberately over the ruins of the old house and stopped near the top of the hill where The Playhouse once stood, at the edge of the woods that were now gone. Pointing to a pile of timbers—all that was left of the little shack—he said to Craig, "Look at that!"

Craig strained to see in the pale moonlight. There was the board with the now-familiar hobo markings, some crossed through. But there was something new! He picked up the broken piece to get more light. There was no mistaking the sign. It now read,

BB IS BACK

Craig gasped deeply as he awoke and sat up, still in his bed. The nightmare was over.

EPILOGUE

Sunlight danced across the Pacific and flooded the lanai with early morning warmth.

"Let's open this baby," Mark was saying to his brother, holding a strongbox that was encrusted with rust. "I need a screwdriver to pry it open."

At this moment, from somewhere inside the house, came the familiar cheerful lilt of two feminine voices, returning Mark and Craig to the here and now. Their wives were up, prompting Craig to glance at his watch.

"Wheee-ooo! Guess what time it is, brah!"

Mark took a startled look at his own watch.

"My God—seven o'clock! We've been out here *all night?*"

Craig's wife Trudi appeared at the screen door and echoed, "Hi, guys! Don't tell me you've been out here all night! How about some breakfast?"

"Sounds great. But first, we want to see what's in this old strongbox— could you get us a screwdriver?" Craig asked.

Maryanne looked over Trudi's shoulder and observed, "You guys really burned the midnight oil—in fact, you're still burning it!" She pointed to the tiki torches, their flames flickering in the gentle morning trades.

Mark rose to extinguish the torches as the foursome chuckled at the witticism.

The men could hear Trudi and Maryanne laughing animatedly and joking about their men needing a screwdriver first thing in the morning. Maryanne returned with the tool and announced that breakfast would be ready in about an hour. She rejoined Trudi in the kitchen.

Mark inserted the tip of the screwdriver under the corroded metal lid and exerted pressure. The rusty lock snapped easily, producing a fine cloud of red dust that settled onto Mark's lap.

"I have a strange feeling about this," he said.

"Whatever's in there, it must have had a special meaning to Dad," Craig commented.

214

"Locked up like this, it had to be something that he didn't want anyone to see. Hmmm—it's a bunch of letters."

"Who from?"

"There's just initials on the envelopes. Let's see—they're all from the same person—'T.N.'"

"What's the postmark?" Craig asked.

"Pretty faded—uh—Helsinki!"

"Wow—they're from Finland! What's the date?"

Mark squinted at the barely legible postmarks. "Looks like—1944 and 1945—yep, they were all written over a one-year period. What say I read them chronologically?"

"All right—which one is first?"

Mark shuffled through them. "This is it—the U.S. postmark is October 1944—forwarded from the Navy Department, just like Ab's letter." Mark looked at the addresses on the other envelopes, and added, "After the first one, they're all addressed to FPO New York, N.Y."

"So he must have written back," Craig deduced. "Well, what are you waiting for? 'Damn the torpedoes—full speed ahead!'" Craig quoted.

Mark withdrew the letter somewhat shakily, wondering what new revelation it might contain. He took a quick look ahead at the signature, and breathed the name.

"Tatiana."

"Hmmm—sounds like the female gender, eh brah?" said Craig.

"Yeah—good ol' Dad! Listen to this:" Mark read aloud.

Dearest Ray,

I pray that you are surviving this terrible war and that this letter finds you safe and well.

Where do I begin? I am living now in Finland, and I am very lucky to be out of the Soviet Union, because there it would not be so good for me.

You see, a trusted friend—from my childhood!—betrayed me. He delivered your message to the KGB, and I very nearly did not escape with my life. I tell you the whole story sometime maybe—if this letter reaches you. But this time I tell what is more important that you know.

215

*We have a baby—I mean you and me. From our great love
exactly nine months later came this beautiful boy. I see your face
when I look at him—I so wish you could see him! The future I am
planning for him will honor you, but he must be a Russian—you
will understand—so I have named him Sergei. I will raise him to
be a leader in ending Communist oppression in the USSR.*

*You must feel no obligation toward me or Sergei. For now I
will remain in Finland and I hope we exchange many letters.
When the war is finally over, I will try to return to my homeland.
Then it will be impossible for us to correspond. Until then, please
write.*

*The memory of our night in Murmansk burns within me.
Forever.*

Tatiana.

"Jesus Christ!" Mark's spontaneous outburst shattered Craig's pensive
silence and caused him to jump in surprise.

"What in the world is going on out there?" Maryanne said to Trudi, as
Mark's epithet resounded throughout the house. Trudi looked up from the
stove where she was tending the eggs.

"Guess we'll hear soon enough. What a time they're having! Did you
hear them last night?"

"*Did* I! I don't think Mark's been up all night since his navy days—forty
years ago—and then, only because he *had* to!"

"I know I haven't seen Craig this excited since their first book hit the New
York Times bestseller list," Trudi added.

The next two letters were fat and contained Tatiana's fascinating account
of her betrayal and subsequent harrowing escape into Finland. Fanning the
air with the pages he had just read, Mark looked up thoughtfully at his
brother.

"You know, Craig, I think there's another bestseller right here in these
letters—but there's something missing."

"Maybe we'll find it in that last letter," Craig said hopefully.

Mark removed the single sheet from the fourth envelope.

"She dated this one: 'October 7, 1945.'"

Dearest Ray,

I hold your latest letter close to my heart. I am so happy you move to large house in small town. It will be so good place to raise your beautiful children.

Now that the war is ended I go home at last. So, this must be final letter I write. You must not try to find me in USSR, for my past must remain unknown.

Only do not forget the name of your son—our son—Sergei Nobolokov. I raise him in my beliefs. He will be a leader of men in the fight for freedom in my beloved homeland.

I wish you long and happy life of joy and contentment. When you think of me, do not be sad, for you are with me in Sergei. As he grows he will know of you, and he will honor you.

I will never love as I have loved you.

Tatiana.

A loud commotion rose from the lanai, and the two women turned again to see what their husbands were up to this time.

"What in heaven—" Trudi exclaimed.

"It couldn't be!" Maryanne was incredulous.

"My God, it must be the 'Indian dance'!"

The two men had joined hands and were jumping up and down and hooting while careening about and turning in circles—exactly as their father and their father's father had done in generations past.

"I've heard them talk about it, but I never knew *they* did it!" Maryanne said.

"I think it's about time we find out just what's going on. Come on!" Trudi said, heading for the lanai with determination.

The two men were thumping in great leaps across the deck, causing it to shake and rumble. The ritual captivated the wives, and they were so vastly entertained that they watched, wide-eyed, until exhaustion began to take its toll and the dance wound down.

Smiling, Trudi finally said, "All right, you two—what's this all about?"

Panting, but grinning widely, Mark turned excitedly to the women. "Pack your bags, girls! We're going to Moscow!"

"What?" came a chorus from Trudi and Maryanne. "*Why?*"

Craig, eyes twinkling, gasped, "You have heard of the great Nobolokov, haven't you?"

"Of course we have," said Trudi, and Maryanne nodded in agreement.

"Well, hang on, girls." Mark drew a deep breath, thrust back his shoulders, and proudly announced, "The president of Free Russia...."

"—The man who led the overthrow of Communism!" Craig inserted, Mark grinning at the contribution.

"—is *our brother!*"

Never were two men more pleased with themselves. The women did not entirely understand—perhaps no one could. They shook their heads and returned to the task of making breakfast, confident that their husbands would fill in the missing details once they came back down to earth. For now, they left them alone, for they were once again lost in wild shouts and gesticulations. Craig paused to speak.

"You know, Mark, I always felt there was more to Dad's War Story than what we heard. Why do you suppose he never looked up Tatiana?"

"Well, we don't know that he didn't. But I think he probably considered it too risky—both for himself and for Tatiana. I wonder if Sergei knows he was fathered by an American!"

"Good point. This could be a bit tricky if we show up and say, 'Hey, our Dad had a liaison with your mother during the war, and guess what?'" Craig laughed.

"Well, it's a new millennium. Russia is a new country now that the last of the hard-line Soviets are gone and the old fear of a communist resurgence is dying. Think of it! We have watched these events with fascination over the years, never knowing how intimately connected we were," Mark said.

"Now I understand why Dad took such an intense interest when Nobolokov rose to power and was elected president. It wasn't just joy at seeing the demise of the Soviet Union—it was pride in his son!" Craig registered satisfaction with his revelation, and Mark nodded thoughtfully. Craig continued, "Our destinies are linked. Puts a whole new perspective on our family history. We ought to call Karl!" Their older brother was the Mosier genealogist.

"He'll want to brush up on his Russian! But let's wait awhile—I want to savor this new feeling."

. . . . .

218

There was a stirring in the air reminiscent of lost youth, of falling cherry blossoms in the springtime, of that mystical timelessness that binds the ages together. They are boys again, playing by the broad lawns on Water Street, where the sidewalk runs down past flowered trellises, and around them is the same air they breathed fifty years ago. It wafts through the green boughs of the trees that are the same trees and disturbs the same puffy dandelions to release their tiny seeds on parachutes to fly across the same grass. Back behind the same pansy rows and the holly trees looms the same big house, standing still like a sentinel. From the porch their mother is calling.

"Maa-ark! Craa-aig! Come in for lunch!"